SCAR

A REVOLUTIONARY WAR TALE

J. ALBERT MANN

CALKINS CREEK
AN IMPRINT OF HIGHLIGHTS
Honesdale, Pennsylvania

Calkins Creek
An Imprint of Highlights
815 Church Street
Honesdale, Pennsylvania 18431
Printed in the United States of America

ISBN: 978-1-62979-465-5 (hc)
ISBN: 978-1-62979-559-1 (e-book)

Library of Congress Control Number: 2015953545

First edition
The text of this book is set in Sabon.
Design by Barbara Grzeslo
Production by Sue Cole
10 9 8 7 6 5 4 3 2 1

*For Judith Brashier, my plucky mother-in-law,
who read my book in its first draft and announced
it was the best book she'd ever read.
Your kindness knew no bounds.*

CHAPTER ONE

THREE DAYS
THURSDAY, JULY 22, 1779

Their screams blind me. I run. Fast. So fast that I run right through my limp. There is nothing I can do for them now— not for Dr. Tusten, not for Mr. Jones or Jon Haskell, not for any of them. Even as I dodge a blur of trees and rocks and branches, the scene under the ledge replays in my mind, Dr. Tusten shouting at me to run, that hatchet . . .

My lame foot catches a rock and I meet the ground. Hard. The musket ball in my stomach shoots searing pain straight up into my teeth.

This can't be happening.

I dig my forehead into the hemlock needles and suck in the familiar smell of soil—I wish I could go back three days in my life, just three days . . .

Something snaps.

I jerk my face from the dirt. There is an Indian half buried in the leaves, lying on his back not more than a yard from me. His chest rises and falls in quick motions. His face is wet from sweat and his clothes are stained with blood.

We stare at each other.

Then I stumble to my feet, looking everywhere at once,

to make sure there are no others pointing muskets at me from behind the pines.

There's no one else.

He raises his hand and swipes at my knees with a hunting knife. His attempt is feeble. Even now, he fights. He looks half dead and yet he lifts that knife, tries to kill. I reach out and snatch the knife away from him. An ache sprouts in my chest like a twisting black vine, wrapping its dark branches around my heart. It is hate, coiling, choking hate. I hate everything. I hate everyone. I hate Dr. Tusten with his knowing eyes. I hate Colonel Hathorn for leaving us. I hate my father for not telling the truth, for not telling me about the blood and the screaming. I hate these woods. And I hate this Indian.

Gripping the knife, I lunge at him. It seems to be what he expects, and he doesn't move to protect himself. Instead, he closes his eyes and waits for me to plunge it into him.

"You fool," I spit, whipping the knife into the dirt. And using my good foot, I kick him as hard as I can. Again. And again. His soft, squirming body hardens everything inside me into cold iron. In my mind I see my fellow soldiers, my neighbors, my friend Josh. I see them lying in these woods, death staring up at the blue sky through the old hemlock branches. I kick and kick and kick . . . Anger runs out of my eyes and nose, it steams out of my skin, specks of it spew from my mouth.

"This is it. This is what I wanted," I cry. "Not to be digging ditches to keep in the chickens on a dusty farm, but to be in Washington's war, to be a Patriot, to be like my father, to be killing, killing, killing."

Dark blood spreads across the Indian's shirt. He lies with his eyes closed, moaning for something or someone, maybe his mother, for he looks like a child curled in the leaves with his hands balled into fists under his chin. What have I done? What have I just done?

I drop to my knees and cover the bloodstain on his shirt with my hands. He moves to push me away, but he's too weak. My head feels like it's filled with flax. "I'm sorry. I'm so sorry," I whisper. The blood won't stop. It keeps coming. I press harder.

The Indian breathes in short, dry gasps. His blood oozes out around my blackened fingernails. He moans small and quiet. His eyes are tightly shut. I need the knapsack.

I stumble to my feet and spin in awkward circles, searching the ground for the doctor's knapsack I'd been carrying before I fell. Behind the rock . . .

As I rip open the bag, the neatness of its contents freezes me. Dr. Tusten had placed each item in so carefully. What a waste of time. But how could he have known that he would never open it again?

I dump the entire bag onto the ground, letting the bottles of iodine and salt roll off into a patch of partridgeberry. I reach for a roll of bandage and a dressing—the very same items I'd climbed to the top of the ledge to find for the doctor. They are so clean. I hesitate, hating to soil them.

The Indian moans.

I grab the bandage and dressing, retrieve the knife, and head back to where the Indian is lying. His eyes are open now, and they follow me. He again says something to himself, like a prayer. I glance down at the knife in my hand. "I'm not going to hurt you," I tell him, but I don't know if he can understand me.

He lies without moving. I pull the muslin shirt from his sticky skin using the beading sewn to his collar. The smell of blood forces itself up my nose and down my throat, gagging me. His stomach is whole.

I search higher, finding the wound, a thin, deep cut of a knife running about the length of my thumb up near his ribs, almost under his armpit. The blood flows faster now that I've freed it.

I wad the square cloth of the dressing the way Dr. Tusten taught me and place it over the pulsing slice in his skin. I think about the iodine lying under the partridgeberry, but decide that cleaning the wound can wait; the blood needs to be stopped. I apply my weight to the balled-up dressing. "I'm stopping the bleeding," I tell him. But I can see from his clenched teeth and tightly shut eyes that he isn't listening, even if he could understand me.

Finally, the blood begins to darken and my dressing is holding back the flow instead of soaking it up. I wait ten counts and decide it has slowed enough that I can crawl out to where I dumped Dr. Tusten's bag. I pluck the rest of the bandages off the forest floor, shaking off the needles and cockleburs stuck to them.

Ripping his shirt in two, I unravel most of it from his body and toss it aside, so I'm able to wrap his injury properly. His shirt resembles mine, except for the red beading sewn to his collar.

He grunts in pain when I lift him to slide the bandage around his body. I need to wind the cloth over his wound, looping it up and behind his other shoulder like a strange spider web. This will keep up the pressure so the bleeding doesn't return. He's looking off into the branches, but I can tell he's watching me. I pretend not to notice as I wrap and listen to the whistles of the chickadees stripping the hemlock cones overhead. I take my time, because when I'm done with this task, I'll have no other.

He shivers. The July sun is finally on its way down, but the air doesn't feel any cooler.

Water. In the fading light, I remove the wooden canteen still strapped to my side that I've been carrying for Josh since this morning. When we were first separated in battle, I'd worried that he would need it, but the musket fire soon made me forget about Josh and his thirst. The water stings my throat and makes my eyes tear. I sit back and drink more. When I'm finished, I slide over to the Indian and raise his head in the growing darkness and bring the canteen to his lips. He tries to help by holding up his head. I push the jug against his mouth, feeling his dry lips with my fingers. He gulps at first, and then, with his thirst mostly quenched, he drinks slowly. I pull the canteen away and he draws in air with less difficulty than before. He

11

shivers again, which makes him moan in pain.

"Are you cold?"

My voice sounds like a stranger's. He doesn't answer. I still have no idea if he understands English. I'm almost sure that, like his commander, Joseph Brant, this boy is Mohawk. But all I can say in Mohawk is *niá:wen*, which means "thank you."

Pushing the peg back into the canteen, I set it down and remove the filthy hunting frock of my father's that I've been sweating in all day, and place it over him. I see his eyes move down me, landing on my shirt. I follow his gaze. The red stain surprises me. I'd forgotten I'd been shot. But now that I've recalled it, I wonder how the terrible sting of the lead could have ever escaped me. I lift my shirt and run my finger over the tiny hole in my stomach where the ball gored its way in. It's still wet in the center. I peel off my shirt and wrap it around my middle, tying it on the opposite side of my wound. The hot air folds itself around my skin. "I wish there were a breeze," I say.

Again, he says nothing.

Moonlight begins to sprinkle the forest floor around us. He looks so small, covered in the frock with only his head and moccasins sticking out from either end. There are pieces of dead leaves and hemlock needles tangled in his scalp lock—the long, thin ponytail that is his only hair. The rest of his head is shaved clean. I can barely make out the features on his face through all the musket powder and war paint.

12

If only my mother were here sitting next to this Indian boy, she'd wash him good.

Whenever one of us became ill, my mother insisted on washing us using her cracked leather bucket and rag while we lay in bed. She said it was proper for the sick to be washed. The night my father died, she balanced on the broken stool next to his bed with her beat-up old bucket and sang his favorite hymn, "Come, O Thou Traveler Unknown," while she scrubbed his tan, bearded face and glowing white arms.

> *Come, O thou Traveler unknown,*
> *Whom still I hold, but cannot see!*
> *My company before is gone,*
> *And I am left alone with Thee.*
> *With Thee all night I mean to stay,*
> *And wrestle till the break of day;*
> *With Thee all night I mean to stay,*
> *And wrestle till the break of day.*

My father entered heaven clean.

I rise, ignoring the flash of pain behind my ribs, and stir up the floor of the forest searching for another dressing. Dumping water onto it from my canteen, I begin to wipe at the boy's dirty forehead. He squirms to avoid me. But I will not be put off. I think my mother would enjoy seeing me do this. It would please her.

The Indian surrenders quickly and allows me to scrub

at him without a fight. I'm more or less smearing the black powder and paint this way and that across his wide face and pointy chin. Although a bit of it seems to be sticking to my dressing. He has closed his eyes.

"It's good to be clean." Again, my own voice sounds so out of place here. I'm only twenty miles upriver from home. Every hemlock and birch looks the same as the trees in the small wood where I've lived my entire life without ever wandering farther than a whisker. But I couldn't feel more separated from my mother and sister right now if I were sitting on one of the stars just turning up in the sky.

I draw in a long, slow breath as I work. The smoke from the musket fire still hanging in the air stings my throat. Pouring more water from the canteen onto the dressing, I wipe at the Indian's cheek and uncover a long, jagged scar running from under his eye down to his jaw. He looks so young, maybe my sister Mary's age, thirteen. It's easy to imagine this boy playing hide-and-seek in the high grass along the river with the other children of his village. I used to love to do that.

I set at washing his neck, but the hooting of an owl has my eyes moving in and out among the dark tree trunks, searching for the movement of an enemy. The thought of finding a comrade doesn't even occur to me. We lost so badly today that I know not to hope for help. Everyone I know is either dead or has long run off.

I think back over the last three days. The memory of Tuesday morning's raid assaults me—hiding under the laurel branches while my home, with its graying pine wood and perfect mud chinking, burned to the ground. Followed by the militia's endless march upriver after our attackers. And finally, I hear it again—that single shot of the musket that started the battle. I squeeze my eyes shut, trying to drive away all thoughts of what happened next.

I guess I could have taken off with the colonel at the battle's end, headed for the river like so many others. Why didn't I? Again, that final scene at the ledge plays in my mind—the approaching chants, the burst of painted faces into the clearing, Dr. Tusten's command, the screaming, that hatchet.

My eyes spring open and scour the deep blackness of the forest all around me, searching for men with hatchets. There is no one.

I breathe, trying to quiet the pounding of my heart's blood in my ears. I look down at the Indian boy beneath my dirty dressing. He looks back at me. I can see thoughts moving through his eyes. What is he thinking? Is he afraid? Can he tell that I am? Does he know that he's dying in the woods with only a sixteen-year-old crippled farm boy to wash his face? Can he tell that's all I am—a crippled farm boy wondering what to do next?

I look away as the last question burns in my stomach next to the musket ball . . .

What am I going to do next?

CHAPTER TWO

WOMEN

TUESDAY, JULY 20, 1779

"Noah!"

My mother is forever shouting at me. She has no patience.

"Noah!"

And I must show myself and answer her, no matter if I'm in the middle of something important or not.

"NOAH!"

I stumble out of the privy, tripping over the daylilies my mother insisted on surrounding it with, and head toward the cabin.

"I'M COMING," I shout. After my father died, I thought I would be the man of the house, but my mother took the job.

"Noah, look at the crib. We're almost out of wood. And we're right in the middle of boiling lye water and pig's grease for soap." She stands in the door, hands on her hips. Her hair is pinned up but falling down in wisps around her face. She is pretty. It always strikes me as odd that someone with so sweet a face can be so . . . competent. "After you fill the crib, wash up. It's almost dinner time." She turns and enters the cabin in a sweep of buntlings.

My mother never stops moving, unless perhaps she's taken up her quilting or is shelling walnuts, but even in those instances, her hands continue to move.

I sigh and turn toward the woodpile. I'm so bone-weary from my long walk yesterday. I walk every evening after my chores. I do it to prove that I can. When I was three years old, a visiting neighbor's horse stepped on my foot, crushing all its bones. My father wanted my foot amputated to save my life. But my mother wrapped it tightly and nursed me through a two-week fever. People said I wouldn't survive. Then they said that I wouldn't walk again. They were wrong on both counts. Or rather, mostly wrong. I do walk, but with a limp. When Mary was a child, she would constantly ask me if it hurt to walk. I told her it didn't. I told her this because it's what I told myself. It did not hurt and I could walk . . . and so I do walk . . . every day.

I walk to the same place, a part of the woods that I call my "farm." A small clearing about a mile southeast of our cabin, which is halfway between our farm and Van Auken's Fort. It's a good spot, closer to the Neversink River than our farm. The land is level and well-drained. The color and depth of the soil are perfect. And as to location for water, it could not be better. The Neversink is a smaller river than the Delaware, but it's filled with trout and bass and carp. It's just a good spot.

I hide a yawn. And then a second one.

I can't look like I'm dragging or my mother will frown the next time I head out for my walk. She has never liked my walks. She knows I walk just to prove I can, and believes that if I'm to tax my foot, it should be in her service, and not for proving points. Not that she has ever allowed me to use my foot as an excuse to get out of chores—just as she doesn't believe in proving points, she also doesn't believe in excuses. Unless of course that excuse is one she favors, because she believes it's perfectly fine to use my foot as an excuse to keep me from joining the war. We never speak of these things, we just frown at each other.

But my walks are mine and I will not give them up. The only time I have my head to myself is on my walks. At least, that used to be the only time. Now, of course, Eliza Little is always sitting at the fork in the path waiting for me. It's like there's a woman everywhere I turn.

"Noah," my mother complains, "we need the crib filled today, not at some point this year."

I load faster. What my foot lacks in strength I more than make up for with my arms. And if I am exhausted, I'm determined that neither my sister nor my mother will see it.

Mary comes to the door of the cabin. Her corset is loose and the sleeves of her white shift are rolled up past her elbows. Her dark hair is pulled tightly up under her cap and her cheeks are bright red from the heat of soap-making. She watches me load. "You look tired today," she says.

Zounds! I cannot hide anything, living with two women. They are always looking straight through me. I miss my father. He would ruffle my hair like I was just a child and shout at the two of them to let me be. Even last year, when I was fifteen. But I never minded it.

"I am not tired," I scowl. "I'm actually full of energy on this beautiful summer day, Mary Elizabeth Daniels."

She laughs at me as she turns back to the iron cooking pot and her soap. Mary is a combination of both our parents. She has the drive and beauty of my mother and the comical spirit of my father. A happy and content girl who sees no reason why everyone else should not be the same. She also sees no reason, even though she is almost three years younger than me, why she shouldn't tell me what to do and when to do it. I throw myself into my chair at the table and smile as broadly as humanly possible. I will *not* let women rule my life.

"Eat," Mary commands, as she places a loaf of rye bread, a tankard of bee balm tea, and a bowl of cornmeal mush in front of me.

And I eat.

CHAPTER THREE

SCAR

THURSDAY, JULY 22, 1779

I look over at the Indian. His breathing is ragged, but steady. I return to staring out at the dark edges of our circle of moonlight. Except for a warm trickle of blood running from my wound, nothing is moving.

I should have run. I should have run for the river like the others. I can't stop searching the woods surrounding us, hoping that I will see someone. But then I dread who that someone might be, and begin to fear any potential movement through the trees. Although after a brief moment of watching and listening, I again wish for anyone to emerge. Yet there is only darkness and the chirping of crickets.

The Indian turns his head to look at me. He's awake.

"Are you thirsty?" I ask. The heat is unbearable. If it would just let up a little, I might be able to think straight. I roll over to search for the canteen and am met by a stabbing through my middle so horrible that my stomach rises right into my throat. I can taste the vomit. I stay on my knees, holding it back. Praying for it to pass. Slowly, too slowly, the pressure in my head and chest releases, the nausea falls away, and I'm able to look about for the canteen.

Finding it, I crawl back to the Indian. He's watching the night sky. I follow his gaze and am struck by how many stars are out. There is more twinkle than there is black sky, the same sky I left at home yesterday morning. But there's no comfort up there. The brightness of the stars has always seemed cold to me. I frown and look back at the boy who has become my patient. The white light of the moon catches on the shiny scar running down his cheek . . . Scar. I will think of him as Scar.

My father named everyone. He rarely called people by their given names, but instead by names he created. The more he liked you, the more names he'd forge. Even our cow had several, since she had both good udders and a quiet temperament. All of my sister's names were of the soft variety: Lamb, Duck, Mouse. I also had many names, but most often I was Cluck, the sound made by our old rooster. My mother had the longest list of us all. But his favorite name for her was "my sweet Wag," which always made my mother smile, for *wag* means "one with a mischievous humor," which she is not.

Kneeling, I once again help Scar raise his head to drink from the canteen. He barely sips at it before he lets his head fall heavy in my hand. "Come on, a little more, try again," I rally. I know his disinterest isn't good. I shake the canteen. We have plenty for tonight, but I'll have to run down to the river at first light for more. I only drink a little, as if in solidarity with him, then close up the canteen and set it down by my side.

But even with the throbbing in my belly pulling at me, I'm not ready yet to retire back to the hot hemlock needles. I spot the emptied knapsack and begin picking everything out of the leaves and dirt, and placing it back inside the sack. As I close it, I'm reminded of how neatly Dr. Tusten had packed it, and I wonder if I, too, will never open it again. I shiver, sending a wave of pain through myself, and I cry out.

Scar looks up. I scoot back to him with the knapsack. His breathing sounds wet. It's not a pleasant sound, and the more I listen to it, the more it seems to fill the quiet woods.

"Everything's fine," I tell him. But my voice is flat and I don't even believe myself. I pick pieces of dead leaves out of his scalp lock and tuck the frock around him. He winces when I move nearer to his wound.

"Let me check it." I lift a corner of the frock. I can see a small dark spot soaking through the middle of the dressing. "I'll rewrap it in the morning. By then the bleeding will have stopped and I'll clean it out well and put fresh linen on it."

His eyes seem to say something. It's the same look that my father's eyes held when he watched me struggle with my schooling. Does he understand me? The Indian turns his head back toward the sky.

"Try again to drink," I tell him, and move for the water. I see him shake his head no. I smile. He does understand me. The Indians we trade with often speak English. And since the Mohawk have been living cheek-by-jowl with the Colonists for over a hundred years, many of them speak it well. "We'll wait on the water," I say, swallowing a groan as I half fall, half

22

roll to the ground next to him. "We should be careful with it, anyway, because I can't get us any more until morning."

This time he doesn't respond, but lies as still as a turtle on a log in the sun, under my father's frock.

That frock . . . My father had been away up north, fighting with General Gates at Saratoga, and had been gone for three months when I saw him walk out of the woods wearing that frock. It was the color that caught my eye, a faded blue, like the sky on a cold winter's afternoon. I screamed for Mary and my mother, and at the same time, took off in my lopsided gallop to greet him. He dropped his load and ran toward me. When we came upon each other, my father jumped into my arms, and under the surprise of his great weight, my legs gave out and we tumbled off the path and into the long grass. I remember shouting at him that he could have smashed my good foot under his large backside. And he just laughed and took my head in both his hands and placed a big wet kiss on my forehead. I told him that he looked like a fat blue sow. That had him howling with laughter. His face was so red and his frock so blue.

And I laughed with him, despite my anger. I had missed him.

I miss him now.

When he returned from Saratoga, he talked of nothing but freedom and revolution. My father was a great Patriot. My mother was not. She kept her head bent over her knitting or ironing—working even harder than she usually did. It was November, two years ago now, and there was plenty to do with winter coming on. While my father split wood and spun his stories, she stayed far away, collecting chestnuts, drying beans and peas, and plucking goose feathers. She hated this talk.

Mary and I loved it. My father's tales would whip up his spirit like cream in a butter churn . . . the declaration of our independence, the battles, the bravery and honor.

Lying here, home and that November day seem so far away.

As does my father.

I can't believe that only two days have passed since I grabbed his frock on my way out of the cabin. How foolish to have gone back for it when I could smell how close the danger was. But I couldn't leave it.

CHAPTER FOUR

THE FROCK
TUESDAY, JULY 20, 1779

I swallow a mouthful of corn mush and look up at Mary. She's looking back at me. We both smell it.

Fire.

Before I can even drop my spoon, my mother is rushing back into the house with her arms full of bed linen. We know what to do. We've been fearing this day. We make for the door, bumping into one another.

Mary and my mother shoot out of the cabin. But I stop short, clutching at the door frame to keep myself from falling over . . . the frock.

Turning and flopping onto the planked floor, I drag my father's hunting frock out from under my mother's bed and stumble back to my feet. In one leap, I'm out the door and loping after my mother and Mary.

We make for the woods to the east of the cabin. The three of us, white-faced and winded, meet at the laurels. After the Indian raid on our neighbors up in Peenpack last October, I dug a wide, shallow ditch in the center of where the laurels are thickest. At the bottom of the ditch, I placed a knife in a leather sack and covered it with dirt.

My mother jumps into the ditch and pulls Mary in with her. I tumble after them, and toss the frock to my mother.

"Why did you bring this?" she asks.

I don't answer. I just start digging for the sack. Pulling it from the dirt, I yank at the drawstring with stiff fingers. Mary grabs it from me and unties the laces and hands it back. Then she drops onto her knees at the top of the ditch and begins searching the woods with her eyes. "I can't tell which direction the smoke is coming from," she whispers. "Can you, Noah?"

I slice through some of the larger branches near us with the knife, too busy to think about the smoke. My mother is gathering the branches piled on the side of the ditch that I'd already cut as part of my weekly chores.

"Maybe it's just a fire, maybe there aren't any Indians coming," Mary says.

I wish it were true, but I can feel them. Or at least I can feel my skin prickling. My mother knows they're coming, too. She lays my father's frock on the ground and pushes Mary down onto it and begins covering her with laurel.

"Mother," I say, turning to hand her branches, "should I make for the fort?"

She doesn't stop burying Mary to answer.

"Mother," I repeat, but I'm interrupted by the shouts of men.

Mary whimpers.

"Don't worry, Mary, they won't find us. Close up your ears with your fingers and talk to Father," I tell her.

There was a time when we didn't fear Indians. But since four of the six nations of the Iroquois joined the British, they've become a vicious enemy. Last October's raid taught us this. On a beautiful fall day, with the sky the color of blue iris and the leaves of the beeches a brighter orange than the tip of a well-tended fire, they whipped through our neighboring settlement, burning everything in sight and murdering anyone who got in the way.

Their cries grow louder. My mother grabs my arm, and the two of us huddle down with Mary in between, covering ourselves with the remaining branches. Just before I bury myself in laurel, I see them come out of the woods north of the cabin. At first my eyes just catch movement through the trees. But then I see the red of war paint.

The whooping and hollering flattens my body against the earth. I can feel Mary shaking. I move closer to her. The smell of burning wood settles into the ditch with us. I know that it's my home that's burning. One Indian in particular shrieks above the rest. It sounds as if he's standing ten yards from us. Mary's body shakes even harder and I'm afraid it will rustle the branches. I move my hand over the dirt slowly to find hers. She grabs my hand. Her nails dig into my skin. I can feel her fear. I can smell it.

"Mary." I say it so softly it comes out like a puff of air. "Mary, put your nose down to Father's frock. Can you smell him? He's here with us. They'll leave soon. It won't be long."

Mary begins to sob. I can't actually hear her crying, but can feel it. I know that movement well. For weeks after Father died, she would come to my bed at night, like when we were small, and slide in next to me. Clutching at my nightclothes, she'd cry silently so that my mother wouldn't wake. Her body rocking back and forth without making a single sound.

There is a loud clap and the three of us jump in unison under our branches. The Indians roar with glee. The roof of our cabin has collapsed. I hear a single voice. He barks out orders in English to search for our animals. I'd released the cows and pigs this morning to forage.

"Mother, I must run to alert others," I whisper. She doesn't say a word, even though I know she heard me. "Mother," I repeat, "they're busy gathering the animals. At least allow me to warn the Van Ettens." The Van Ettens are our closest neighbors, living just northwest of us. South of the Van Ettens, and directly west of our farm, are the Van Fleets, who live halfway between us and Van Auken's Fort.

"You know I can make it in less time than it will take them to find the pigs."

She says nothing, although she has spoken . . . silently.

I can hear the cows bellowing, complaining loudly about having to move in the midday heat. It sounds like many of the men have gone on ahead, leaving a few behind to drive the beasts. Mary's breathing slows. She thinks we're out of danger; they're leaving. But I want to be sure. We're safe here, and I feel we should not come out of our hole for quite a long time. Maybe even wait for early evening.

Mary interrupts my thoughts. "They're leaving, Noah," she whispers.

"Be still, Mary," I squeeze her hand and she relaxes a little.

I settle more comfortably onto the dirt and stare off through the branches at the treetops and the small amount of sky that I can see. What a strange view of the world this is, lying in a ditch covered with brush.

I can smell our house still burning. Will anything be left? All our clothes and bedding will be gone, along with my father's small library of hymnals. My mother's Bible, too.

My mother reads her Bible as often as she can. She started after Father died. The night he passed, she picked up that book and started to read. I figured she was looking for answers. How could a strong man catch a cold, and a week later, be dead? And how were we supposed to live without him? She must not have found the answers right away, because she kept reading. I didn't like it. My mother never needed help with anything.

I can feel Mary's body moving evenly. I turn my head to look at her. Her eyes are closed, and whatever thoughts are in her mind seem far away from here. She looks sweet. I watch her for a few minutes, and then I think of someone else . . . Eliza Little.

I start to sweat. Is the Littles' farm close enough for them to have heard the Indians' yelling? How could they not have heard? And, just like us, they must have smelled the fire.

There is a light snap. My body goes rigid. Someone is still out there.

My eyes scour the small amount of the world available

to me. My ears work so hard that they ache from the lack of sound.

I see his feet.

My mother sucks in a small breath—she sees them, too.

Oh, Father, please help us, I chant in my head. But I worry that whoever is out there might be able to hear my thoughts. I stop.

I can see his moccasins clearly now. They're highly decorated, with white glass beads sewn to the ankles and each lace ending in a red tassel. He can't be more than five feet from us. Is he looking for us? Maybe he's looking for one of the pigs, or maybe he was lagging behind and got lost. Perhaps he's trying to decide the right way to go. Mary rests peacefully, while the sweat pours out of me like a river in springtime.

The knife. I feel it next to my thigh. I don't want to move in case the branches make any rustling noises. I want that knife. I can't reach down now, but if he begins to check our laurel branches, I'll grab it, dive out, and stab him. Maybe I can kill him before he kills me. I just hope that I can move fast enough after having lain so long in this ditch.

I've never killed anyone, although I've slaughtered many a pig. My father was an expert hunter and trapper, but he hated the slaughtering. Somehow he felt that hunting and trapping was different, more of an even game than walking over to the sow pen with an ax. My mother was actually the expert when it came to sticking the pig. I should hand my mother the knife. I know she wouldn't even hesitate if it meant keeping Mary and me safe. *I can kill him*, I tell myself. *I can do it.*

If I don't kill him, he'll surely scalp me, just as the Tories and Indians did to old Philip Swartwout and his two sons that day last October. The thought of Mary at the mercy of the owner of these moccasins heats my blood, and my muscles strain to break free of the ditch . . . to use the knife.

It's as if the moccasins feel my readiness, because they begin to move away. I keep watching the spot where I last saw them until my sight darkens from the effort.

I drop my head to Father's frock and breathe deeply. I can smell him perfectly. "Thank you, Father," I whisper.

CHAPTER FIVE

SOMEHOW I CAN CHANGE MY FATE

THURSDAY, JULY 22, 1779

Scar cries out from the middle of a deep sleep. I shoot up, only to collapse back to the earth with my guts on fire. What a pair the two of us are. I would laugh, if it weren't for the fact that it isn't very funny.

Scar is silent again. I sink into the forest floor, the throbbing of the ball ebbing with every breath. I have to keep my wits. I'm in better condition than Scar and must be the one to fetch water, and perhaps a little food, in the morning. I should start to think about how I'll move him, too. We can't stay in the woods forever. Maybe I'll find some of our men down by the river. Maybe I'll find some of Scar's. Before I can really think about this, Scar cries out again.

I roll over and push up off the ground, managing to climb to my knees. Hunching over to keep from disturbing the musket ball, I scoot toward him. He's calling to someone in his language. Words fly out of him in short, loud bursts. It sounds like he's trying to explain something. I can't make out anything he's saying.

I lean over his face and try to bring him back to me. "Scar, Scar, it's Noah," but this is ridiculous, of course he

32

doesn't know my name or the name I made up for him. His strange words come faster and his hysteria grows.

"Scar!" I pick up his hand. "Scar!" Ridiculous or not, it makes me feel more secure to call him by my made-up name. "You're all right, Scar."

He continues his babbling. His breathing is back to a wet gurgle. His eyes won't focus. I don't like this. I want him to stop.

I put down his hand and crawl for the canteen, the pain stealing my breath . . . my sight. I tell myself that it hurts so badly because I'm tired. All I need is a little rest. I'll be better by morning.

My knee finds the canteen. Yanking it open, I return to his side and try to make him drink. But it's impossible. He won't have anything to do with it. Pulling the dressing from the waist of my trousers, I dump water on it and wipe the sweat from Scar's face. He shivers and continues to mutter frantically, like he's begging me, or someone, for something.

"I'm here, Scar, I'm right here. Remember me?" I put my face into his. He stops and seems to see me. I try to take advantage of the moment. "Scar, it's me, remember? My name is Noah, Nooo-ahhh," I tell him slowly. "I'm going to take care of you. In the morning I'll bring us water from the river, and maybe search out some food." I remember that most of the militia was carrying journey cake, bread, cherries, figs, and the like. I'm sure I can find one of our sacks abandoned in the woods. My mind instantly turns to what else I might find in the woods—those who did not willingly abandon their sacks. But my thoughts are interrupted by Scar's howls echoing against my chest.

"Please," I plead, "everything is fine."

But it's not fine. This is not a good thing, this madness. I almost feel like joining him in losing all sense. It has got to feel better than this cold tingling blowing through me. I don't know what to do. But I can't listen to this much longer.

I look out into the night. I can only see a few feet in all directions. I begin to imagine what could be hiding just beyond my line of sight, like the long barrel of a musket pointed at my head, or the raised, sharp blade of a hatchet— or worse, wolves. And if these imaginings of mine don't know we're here, Scar's incessant prattle will surely alert them. He has to stop.

I grab him by the shoulders and give him a shake. I mean to shake him gently, but out of fear, I do it violently, shouting right into his face.

"SCAR!"

He screams so loudly that I stumble backward, covered in goose bumps and sweat. My stomach rolls. "No," I whisper, but it's useless to try and stop it. I quickly drag myself away from him. My chest heaves, and it's like I'm being gored by a hundred hot bayonets, and I vomit . . . and vomit.

I haven't eaten anything since yesterday morning, and even then, it was only some dried beans and a little bread, so my body wrenches over and over, calling forth nothing.

I cry out to my mother.

If only I were a child again. I would be home vomiting

into my mother's porcelain bowl, the one she received as a wedding present from my grandmother. My mother always said that it wasn't useful for anything else. She'd rub my back and whisper into my ear as I was sick. I try to think what it was she whispered. But I can't remember. I can't remember anything right now. I'm on my hands and knees, my body shaking, my elbows threatening to unlock and drop me right into the dead leaves. And all I know is the terrible heaving.

After what feels like ten Sunday sermons in a row, the nausea passes. I wait, panting, still on my hands and knees, the fear of it returning swirling around my head like a cloud of gnats. A breeze washes over my burning face, cooling it. It's like a gift straight from God and it gives me the strength to move.

I wipe myself with the dirty dressing and make a note in my head to dig out another one from Dr. Tusten's sack. I like the idea of searching for a clean dressing because it forces me back into the knapsack, putting to rest the idea that I will never open it again. This makes me laugh. How foolish I am—believing that somehow I can change my fate if I can find a real reason to open that knapsack. I laugh harder. I've been through so much in the last few days, and it feels good to allow the heaviness to lift.

But I've forgotten about poor Scar.

I shuffle back to his side and am shocked when his eyes meet mine. He is back. The madness is over.

"How do you fare?" I ask.

His lips tighten. He won't speak.

That's fine. I understand.

"My name is Noah." I pick up his hand in mine and gently shake it. He nods with his eyes. It's enough for me. The fear is gone, with the contents of my stomach. I lie down next to him and wait for the burning in my belly to cool.

Within a few moments, Scar begins to moan again. His moaning has a different tone than before, but I'm still wary. I can't bear another episode. I tell myself to sing. When Mary or I were injured or very ill, my mother or father would sing to us. They both had beautiful voices. My mother has a scratchy voice with a twang that makes you forget the day's toils. And my father had a melodic one that filled you with energy and begged you to join in with him. But every time I did, Mary would laugh. "Some people weren't meant to sing," she'd say.

Scar's moans grow louder. *Think*, I tell myself . . . *tell him a story*. My father always said that a good story was nature's painkiller, better even than peppermint for a toothache. But I don't have a good story. I don't even have a bad one. My father was an excellent storyteller. I know a few of his stories word for word. But they were *his* stories and I can't tell them like he could—with excited spit flying from his lips and his eyes lit up like the first flames leaping from a smoking pile of tinder.

My mind runs through some of the latest gossip in our village. But there isn't anything interesting to repeat—old Mrs. Wheaten had lately entertained using candles that gave off smoke, or there was Mr. Adams, who took "to sip" one evening and ended up sleeping with his chickens.

Scar begins to panic, thrashing about in the pine needles.

I call out to him. "Scar!"

Poorly made candles and farmers disguised by drink aren't going to help this boy forget his injuries. Not too much happens on a hardscrabble farm on a small settlement. But then I remember the day that *she* happened.

"I met her a few months ago," I begin.

Scar does not pay me a speck of attention, but I proceed with my storytelling.

"She came down from Cushetunk, that's probably not that far from here, maybe ten miles north, right upriver. And now that I think about it, she is pretty much all your fault."

He quiets.

"The Tories were stirring up trouble and her father heard that our settlement had soldiers staying with us, and thought his family should spend the rest of the war somewhere safe. I guess that's ironic, because it turned out not to be so safe after all." I stop for a moment, wondering if he's even listening. But no matter if he is, it feels good to be speaking—and not thinking about blood and pain.

"People assumed she and I would become friends when they found out that we were the same age. But those people didn't know me . . . and they certainly didn't know Eliza Little."

CHAPTER SIX

THE STORY OF ELIZA LITTLE

SPRING 1779

"The church service had begun that morning as usual. I remember I'd stood for the hymn but refused to sing. I didn't have the spirit. Not only was the entire sermon still before me, but the whole war had just headed south and left me behind. All the men General Washington sent to the frontier for our protection after last October's raid were now gone. Count Pulaski's dragoons were the first to leave, pulling out in December because they could not keep their horses fed through our long winter. And less than two months after this, his infantry was called away. Finally, in April, even General Hand's infantry was ordered elsewhere. I had planned on joining Hand's infantry, but . . ."

I hesitate. Trying to explain my foot or my mother to Scar would be impossible.

". . . there I was instead, stuck between my mother and my sister in a church pew. Everything was irking me that morning. My neighbor Mrs. Decker's endless chatter to my mother about late frosts and what a nuisance it was to have to cover the corn saplings. My sister Mary's constant humming. The Reverend taking ten eternities to embark on his sermon. Every single person in the congregation with their sniffling and coughing and throat-clearing. I was miserable.

"That's when I heard the church door open. A latecomer. Yet another annoyance. Now the Reverend would have to wait until this dawdler got settled. I turned to see who it was so I could direct my anger accordingly. But the transgressor was someone I'd never seen before in my life.

"Her hair was long and black and tied up by a blue ribbon. She wore a brown gown and a blue petticoat. And she held the hands of two little girls, one on either side of her. It wasn't so often that new people came into our settlement. In fact, besides the troops, it almost never happened at all. I watched her take a seat in an empty pew directly across from us.

"I didn't listen to one word the Reverend said after that. This girl took up all the room in my head. I could tell she was my age, although I would soon learn just how close in age we were. And she was alone with the children.

"When the sermon finally came to an end, I planned to follow her out so that I might hear who she was. But at the opportune moment, my mother remembered a recipe for stewing eel that she needed to impart to Mrs. Decker before she could think to take another step. And although I believe no one needs another recipe for stewed eel, Mrs. Decker decided that she did. Since it would be improper to leave my mother in the pew, I was trapped.

"I watched the girl walk down the aisle and depart the church. Which . . . was fine. It wasn't like I wouldn't hear the gossip on these three girls from Mrs. Decker or Mrs. Van Etten soon enough. But then Mary asked me who they were and I could tell how badly she wanted to know. So for my sister's sake, I attempted to rush us out.

"Until that morning, I hadn't realized how many old people we had in our congregation, and at the moment, they were all in front of us. I tried grabbing onto Mrs. Park's elbow to hurry her along. She generously thanked me for my help while rambling on about growing old and feeble and how I shouldn't let it happen to me. She kept smiling, too, making me feel wicked for wanting to drop her elbow and run. Meanwhile, Mary pushed past me at the doors.

"Finally released from the church, I spotted the girl standing on a small hill in the churchyard with Mr. and Mrs. Van Etten. When I looked over at her . . . she was looking right back at me."

Recalling the moment unsettles me. Even here—in this wild and lonely place—she is able to creep inside me and steal my peace. My hand moves to wipe my brow and I find my forehead hotter than a kettle hanging low on the lug pole. It's like the memory of her eyes have brought on a fever. Swallowing, I press on.

"The girl's stare compelled me to seek occupation. I turned to my mother, but she wasn't behind me anymore. She, Mary, and Mrs. Decker were already making their way up the hill toward the girl and the Van Ettens.

"That's when I spotted Mr. Decker and headed toward him. Martinus Decker is an important man in our settlement and was a good friend of my father's. He and the Reverend were deep in conversation. I knew what they would be talking about before I got there—the war. It's all Mr. Decker ever speaks of. And when I arrived at their side, I found I was correct. The Reverend was grumbling over the loss of troops on our frontier. Mr. Decker was, of course, agreeing. When they noticed me, Mr. Decker clapped me on the back in a friendly way, and the Reverend asked after my family.

"I reported we were well and then stood quietly by, allowing them to return to their conversation. I was happy to be a part of their group while free to have my own thoughts. Every so often I glanced across the crowded churchyard at the girl. There were many of us milling about that Sunday due to the warm spring sunshine."

I look around our clearing. Dark. Quiet. Still. This place doesn't feel as though it shares the same earth as that bright, busy churchyard. I turn to Scar and am surprised when I meet his opened eyes. I suspect I've been silent too long, because he gives me a look that says, Go on.

He's listening.

"When I next checked on the girl, she wasn't there. That's when I caught sight of Mrs. Decker leading the group of them down the hill toward us like a goose leads her goslings to the water's edge. And for some reason, I didn't want to be there when they arrived. But Mr. Decker was engrossed in a new debate with the Reverend, and when I tried to excuse myself, neither paid me any attention. And to walk away without excusing myself would be rude. Although, truth be told, I had no excuse to give, anyway.

"So the girl got closer and closer. And with each approaching step she took, another meaningful thought took flight from my head. By the time she reached us, I swear I could hear the wind whistling through my empty skull.

"Mrs. Decker introduced her to Mr. Decker. It was the first time I heard her name . . . Eliza Little.

"Mrs. Decker explained that Eliza Little had come down from Cushetunk two days before with her father and three sisters. She informed her husband that the Littles were fierce Patriots, and that the Tories were stirring up trouble in the north, so Eliza's father thought it best to surround himself with friends until the war was over. Mr. Decker shook Eliza's hand and expressed his pleasure in meeting her. He then began to enquire after possible shared acquaintances in the north. I was less than a cubit from her but I seemed able to see her only in small pieces—her eyes, her mouth, her hair. Suddenly I heard Mrs. Decker saying my name: '. . . Noah Daniels, Mary's older brother. He is sixteen as well.'"

Scar is coughing.

I break off my story and wait.

He settles.

"Mrs. Decker went on some about how close we lived to each other, and how she was sure we'd all be great friends in no time, but I wasn't listening—mostly because Mrs. Decker always used too many words, but also because Eliza Little reached out to shake my hand. She had to lean forward and pluck my hand from where it hung at my side, because like a fool, I hadn't moved. I shook her hand, and kept shaking it. I meant to . . ."

He's coughing again.

His coughs turn into gasps.

I drag myself to my knees, ignoring the musket ball screaming in my gut. He can't breathe. He's choking.

I rip off the frock and try to sit him up. But the coughing and sputtering are joined by loud, grunting screams when I bend him at the waist. I lay him back down and grab the canteen. "Here," I tell him, trying to force him to drink. The water is the only thing I can think to do. He refuses it and, instead, hacks and chokes. I grab him and, holding his head in one arm, I press the jug to his lips. He fights me. I try again, and succeed in dumping a little water down his throat. But he coughs it right back up, along with a trickle of dark saliva, which runs down his chin.

This is bad.

I crawl to the knapsack for a fresh dressing, with one hand clutching at the lead ball in my stomach to keep it quiet. Scar sputters and hacks behind me. It's a terrifying sound.

There are no fresh dressings.

I untie my shirt and whip it about to remove the leaves and needles. Finding the cleanest corner I can, I tear it off. The air feels cool on my wound. I don't like it. I crawl back to Scar.

It seems something is stuck in his throat, but how can that be? He hasn't eaten anything since I've been with him. I wet the clean piece of shirt using only a small amount of water—we're getting low—and wipe the sweat from his face. Then I sit helplessly by and watch him choke.

I can't stand it. It's like his eyes are growing bigger and his skin is shrinking away from his face. He looks older than when I first found him late this afternoon. Like a tiny old man. And he will not stop choking. He can't cough properly.

What do I do? What do I do? If I could just make him sit up . . .

I try again to force him to sit, but he thrashes at me, and between his surprising strength and my feverish head, I'm unsuccessful.

"You'll choke to death if you don't sit," I yell. But as I'm yelling, I have an idea. And having an idea livens me up. I place him back down, roll him like a log onto his uninjured side, and begin to pound on his back. I've seen the women do this in church with babies. I know Scar doesn't have to belch, but whatever is stuck will have an easier time coming out if I help.

44

Scar can barely draw breath, let alone cough. I pound his back and shout at him. "Cough, Scar, cough!" This poor boy probably wishes I had stabbed him dead this afternoon. But I don't quit. "For the Lord's sake, COUGH!"

Finally, he half spits, half coughs out a thick, dark-brown liquid. Is it vomit? What is it? I move closer. It looks like he's vomited a wet mess of finely ground tea leaves.

Scar is limp with exhaustion, but able to breathe. The coughing has stopped. I roll him back and he sighs in relief. Covering him up, I reach for the water. He's too tired to fight me, and he drinks. I'm so thirsty, but I close the canteen. After I lay his head down, his moon-shadow is out of the way of his vomit and I see it's not tea leaves, but blood he's been choking on. It looks partially dried somehow. But it's definitely blood.

It's then that it hits me . . . He isn't going to live.

I guess I knew this when I first found him this afternoon.

Without thinking, I pick up his hand in mine and look up at the sky between the branches of the hemlock trees. Why is it that when we want answers we know we can't have, we turn our faces to the sky? Maybe it's all those stars. Maybe just comparing our concerns to their twinkling masses shrinks our problems.

Scar squeezes my hand.

I'm afraid to look at him. I know that he knows he's dying.

He squeezes my hand again.

I look down. His eyes are like the stars, full of twinkle.

I'm amazed by how well I know his eyes when I don't even know his name.

"Hand prisoner?" he croaks.

His voice shocks me, and I can barely take in that he spoke, let alone understand his meaning.

"Girl?" he says. "Hand prisoner?"

"What?" I say. "I wasn't holding her hand prisoner. Maybe it was her fault. Maybe she forgot to remove her hand from mine." But then I grin a little sheepishly. "You're right. I held her hand too long," I admit, lying back down next to him. "She had to eventually yank it from me."

He laughs. It's a good sound. *Hand prisoner.* I think Scar might be funny. I like knowing this about him.

"After she released herself from my grip, she said she needed to locate her sisters and head home. Her father was unwell and her older sister needed help in caring for him. As she turned to leave, she stopped and spoke to me: 'So, we are both sixteen. When is the day of your birth?'

"I knew the answer to this, of course, and was just about to give it when my sister answered for me. 'March seventh,' Mary said.

"'I'm the fifth,' the girl said. 'Of course this means I'm the elder, and therefore the wiser, of us.'

"She laughed.

"I didn't.

"'Two days is hardly time to become wise,' I told her.

"She laughed again, although I didn't think what I'd said was funny.

"My mother interrupted our conversation with an invitation for her family to join us for supper the following Saturday when her father was feeling better. She thanked my mother and accepted. After this, she gathered her sisters and left.

"For the next week I worked our farm like a true descendant of my headstrong mother. It being spring, there was a never-ending list of things to do. Fields to prepare, seeds to sow, animals to feed, traps to check. Within the week, I had our small farm looking quite acceptable. I labored at such a pace that when I hit my straw at night, I was already asleep. I wanted to show Eliza Little that those two days she held over me meant nothing.

"When I awoke on the following Saturday, I made a list in my head of a hundred chores to do to keep from thinking about our supper guests. I was cleaning out the smokehouse, number four on my list, and sweating like a pack mule, when Mary came out and told me to clean up for dinner, our midday meal, for we had a guest.

"I never asked who it was. I assumed it was Mrs. Van Etten. She often visits my mother. She's a kind woman, although she speaks too much of her health. I quickly cleaned myself using a dirty rag hanging in the barn and went to dinner. When I stepped into the cabin I bumped right into Eliza Little. And though she tried to hide it, I saw her sniff.

I'm sure I smelled like last year's smoked pork butt."

"Or maybe, smell fish," Scar says, pulling his hand from under the frock and making it swim.

"Yes, thank you," I tell him, "or maybe I smelled like old fish . . . anyway . . . She and her little sisters had come to inform us that their father wasn't feeling well enough for supper that evening, and my mother invited the three of them to stay for dinner."

"Beside noticing how badly I smelled, it was also the first time Eliza Little noticed my foot."

I raise my twisted, thick ankle into the air for Scar to see— the toe end of my moccasin bending awkwardly left.

"And when she noticed, she did something that no one had ever done before . . . She asked me about it. 'Cow, horse, or tree?' she said. When I didn't answer, she answered herself with a shrug and a laugh: 'No matter, all three are the same— useful, but heavy when they land.'

"It was a true statement, so I told her as much. And again, she laughed.

"We sat for dinner over beef mixed with currant and cabbage. And this is where I first learned how much Eliza Little loved to talk. As we ate, she described life in their old settlement, including how they'd lost their mother to the pox the year before. But mostly she entertained us with stories about her older sister Sarah's bad cooking. I'd never seen my mother enjoy herself so much.

"When dinner was finished, my mother and Mary offered to introduce her sisters to our new litter of pigs. Eliza Little and I cleared the table together. It was the first time I'd been alone with her. She told me she was sorry for the loss of my father. I told her I was sorry for the loss of her mother. She stopped clearing then and smiled at me. Not knowing how to respond, I nodded my head. She laughed and called me a serious fellow. But she said it as though being serious was not quite a proper thing. At that moment, my mother came in with fresh water and I announced that I'd walk the girls home. I was determined to behave well no matter what this girl called me.

"On that walk we had our first fight . . . of many. The argument was over the planting of wheat. She believed in growing more wheat than one needed, and then transporting the excess wheat and flour to market. Now, as a matter of course, I'm not against growing more wheat than is necessary to barter for tools and livestock, but to go hauling it about the colonies . . . Never mind, it was a heated fight. And about wheat. Who fights about wheat?"

I turn to Scar. He clearly agrees. Although I know he's humoring me. Mohawk men do not plant wheat. They hunt and fish and fight. Farming is women's work.

. . .

"And that is what I said to her. 'Who fights over wheat?' And do you know what she did?"

I don't wait for Scar to respond.

"Of course, she laughed. She seemed to think everything was funny. Just as she thought that everything needed to be discussed . . . at length. And so we fought, at every meeting, and on every subject—over how much corn to feed a hog through winter—whether grass be cut easiest by sickle or scythe—how to plow a straight row—even what a correctly plowed straight row should look like!

"And if I ever came close to winning one of these arguments, Eliza Little would bring up those extra two days that she'd lived in this world like they were indisputable evidence of her being right about everything. Sometimes she wouldn't even say a word, she'd just smile while she held up two fingers in the middle of my sentence. It made me want to pluck her up and toss her in the Neversink."

My voice is tiring. I try to soothe it with spit, but I have none.

"When we arrived at Eliza Little's home, I excused myself, informing her that I needed to return immediately to complete my chores before dark. She smiled and whispered, 'So serious.'

"That night I lay on my straw, frowning when I thought

50

about Eliza Little—which made me think that perhaps she was right and I was too serious. She did this to me . . . sent my thoughts spinning in frustrating circles. And I slept very little before it was time to rise for church the next day.

"Of course, Eliza Little and her sisters were again at the service. The sermon flew by. I had never known the Reverend to speak so well. It was another beautiful spring Sunday, and when I stepped outside, I saw that she was standing in a group next to Mr. Decker. At first I looked around for others I could speak with. But I decided right then and there that I was going to live the same way I did before Eliza Little arrived. So I walked straight for Mr. Decker to say good morning. He halted his conversation and greeted me with his usual enthusiasm. He then began to introduce me to Eliza Little, forgetting that we had met the previous week, standing right beside him. Before I could stop him, he started in on my excellent character, and what a hard worker I was. If I had written a script in my own hand, I couldn't have done a better job singing my praises. The speech went on for quite a while and I felt I should applaud when he finished. *Take that*, I thought, *two days older and wiser*.

"Eliza Little smiled and told Mr. Decker that she also believed me to be of steady character. But even though the words 'steady character' seemed meant in a complimentary way, I could not take them as such. Instead, I could hear her voice in my head now calling me 'so steady.' How she got into my head, I do not know.

"She then wished us a good day, saying she needed to be

on her way. And before I could stop myself, I offered to see her safely home . . . revealing more of my steady character."

"You see?" I say. "How bothersome she is. And trust me, I had not provoked this from her in any way."

"Woman comes from sky," Scar whispers. "Many times, men ask birds, when you take back woman?"

We turn to each other and laugh.

"A flock of crows," I tell him, "and all my problems might be solved."

All my problems . . . Scar is weakening by the moment and my own cheeks glow with fever. We need more than birds.

"I was once again locked into the task of walking her home when it was the last thing I wanted to do.

"The walk started off quite slowly, for her little sisters needed to dart here and there before they moved in a forward direction—like two busy butterflies. And while the little ones flitted about, Eliza Little engaged in her affection for speech. She told me how they had come from Connecticut when she was a baby because her father had a dream of owning his own farm. About how hard they all had worked for that dream and how her mother had basically died for it. She proudly showed me her fingernails, black with dirt from spring planting. She joyfully spoke of our rich soil, our freezing winters, our sweaty summers. And on top of one particular hill, she even threw open her arms and declared her devotion to the entire river valley.

"I don't know why I did it—maybe it was her passion for the seasons, or maybe her dirty fingernails—but I took her on my secret walk to a certain small patch of land. I'd never invited anyone there before, not even my sister, Mary.

"Her little sisters were thrilled to leave the road for adventure. They engaged me in constant conversation for the entire walk to what I like to call my farm. I explained my plans for the cabin I would build one day and where I would place my barn and fields, and what I would plant first. The butterflies stopped listening when I became invested in the subject of chinking—the mixture applied between the logs in a cabin in order to keep the wind from howling in. Eliza Little didn't stop listening. And she was not shy regarding what she believed were the proper chinking proportions between deer hair, mud, and lime. I actually thought her way too concerned with the lime. But wanting to be polite, I did not mention this at the time.

"When we arrived at my farm, Eliza Little exclaimed over the soil as it crumbled rich and dark between her fingers, pointed out the location's excellence in regard to water, and noted the perfect view in all directions. It made me feel as though I had created the soil and view myself. I told her that I had scouted out this place long ago and that I visited it every evening after my chores were finished. Although as soon as we took a seat together on a rock at the southeastern corner of my farm, we promptly began to fight over how many trees would need to come down, and where was the best placement for the cabin.

"Every day after this, Eliza Little met me on the walk to my farm at the fork in the path between our land and her family's . . . and our fighting continued. We agreed on almost nothing but those things that were at the most elemental level, like building the cabin with its back to the wind. It was so rare that we agreed on anything, that when we did, it felt odd, like a bath in midwinter, and we quickly moved past it."

"You're probably wondering why I even let her walk with me. It's only because she would be standing there at our usual meeting place carrying a birch basket of gingerbread or cranberry tarts. Cranberry tarts . . . What could I do? Of course I had to let her come."

I sigh, picturing Eliza Little the last time I saw her. She wasn't holding onto a basket full of tarts, but holding back a heart full of tears.

Breathing in the smell of the river deeply through my nose—the clean scent of drying stone—I look over at Scar. He is sound asleep.

I wonder if Eliza Little is sleeping right now.

CHAPTER SEVEN

ONE FIELD OF CORN
TUESDAY, JULY 20, 1779

We've been in this ditch far too long. My mother is quiet. Mary is sleeping. The late July sun beats through the branches. I'm covered in dirt and sweat and every part of me itches and aches. Even my mind is uncomfortable as it brings up the faces of my neighbors over and over again. There is a growing dread inside me. I twitch, and a laurel branch sticks into my backside. How would Mr. Decker feel about me lying buried in a hole all day?

I know the answer to my question. Foot or no foot, Mr. Decker would already have me fighting in this war. After my father passed away, I tried to join the militia. Mr. Decker was in favor of it. My mother was not. But even Mr. Decker— a passionate Patriot and an old family friend—was no match for my mother. I hate to admit that I, too, was no match for her.

When my mother refused to allow me to join, Mr. Decker attempted to explain her decision away. He said we couldn't have all our best men off with General Washington, leaving our homes wide open to attack.

Well, today is just that situation. This settlement needs

me and I've chosen to dawdle away in a ditch. How long will I allow myself to be buried under a heap of laurel branches?

I'm about to suggest we climb out when I hear a voice in the distance calling our names.

"Mother, do you hear that?" I ask.

"Yes," she replies.

I venture to move but am too stiff to do more than roll about in the dirt.

My mother struggles to her knees and begins to unbury Mary from the branches. "Mary," she whispers gently in my sleeping sister's ear. "Mary, everything is fine. Wake up now, dear."

Mary slowly opens her eyes and blinks at us in confusion. But when she remembers where we are, her eyes widen with panic and she scrambles to look around herself. My mother grabs her and speaks sternly into her face. "We're safe . . . they're gone."

The calling voice is moving closer. I recognize it as Mr. Van Etten's. We've seen him often of late, since he must pass our farm to visit with his good friend Mr. Little.

The thought of the Littles has me on my feet.

I pluck up my father's frock from the ditch floor and scramble out, sending branches flying.

"Noah, calm down," my mother says. "You'll scare Mary."

"I'll run on ahead and tell him we're fine," I say.

I throw on the frock and start out of the woods as fast

as I can, which is not that fast, because my legs and back still feel like wet wood from lack of use.

I make the clearing just as Mr. Van Etten disappears around the side of a smoking heap of blackened wood. The sight stuns me. It's my home. Or rather, it was.

Mary and my mother come out of the woods behind me.

"There's nothing left," I whisper, choking on the words.

"We're left," my mother says.

Mary leans her head against my arm and takes my mother's hand. We remain like this, staring at the strange sight of our hearth exposed to the summer sky, until Mr. Van Etten appears around the other side of the rubble. I see him jump with joy when he catches sight of us, as much as a man of almost seventy can jump. The three of us start toward him, stumbling over each other's feet because we're walking too closely to one another.

"The Lord have mercy on us all," Mr. Van Etten says in greeting. And he wraps Mary and my mother in an awkward hug. Mary breaks down into sobs. My chest aches with the effort of taking in the sight of everything I've ever known swiftly turning to ash, while listening to the sound of my sister's wretched crying.

"Come, come now," the old man says, wiping her face with his filthy shirtsleeve. Perhaps he, too, has spent time in a ditch today. "Let us be off, there is nothing left here to do. You can pick through it tomorrow after a meal and some sleep."

"Mr. Van Etten, sir, has anyone in the settlement been hurt?" I ask. "Do you know? Do you know how everyone is?" Although there is only one face in my mind.

I can tell he's heard me. But instead of answering right away, he shuffles some, seeming to need a moment to gather his thoughts. Something is wrong. "Well, then," he says, finally, "I was down at the Littles' when the devils came through. Gone by there early this morning to look at a sick sow, I did."

He was at the Littles'.

I suddenly feel unwell. Mr. Van Etten keeps speaking, but I don't hear any of it. And although my eyes are open, they see only the thoughts in my head where I'm whispering a hundred promises to God to ensure everyone's safety . . . her safety.

"She was mighty unsociable and keeping close to the barn during the day . . ."

He's talking about the sow. Why will he not say what happened? Why won't he tell me whether she's alive or dead? It's my fault if any harm has come to her. I should have run to warn everyone, to warn her. How dare I dream of fighting in this war when I can't even crawl out of a ditch on my own? Perhaps my mother is right to hold me back like a child.

"He'd been feeding her mash, you know," Mr. Van Etten continues.

I try to be patient, but we're sucking in the smoke from the blackened remains of my life and Mr. Van Etten is describing what best to feed a sick pig.

"Sir," I interrupt, taking a step closer to him. "How are they, the Littles, sir, and Mrs. Van Etten? How are they, sir?"

"Mrs. Van Etten is fine, boy," he answers. "She was out gathering blackberries and fled to the Van Fleets'. But they were burned out there, too, so she made her way down to the Littles' to find me. But the Littles . . . why," he frowns, "the Littles aren't doing so well."

I have this incredible urge to run. "Tell me," I say, looking directly into his watery eyes. But it's her eyes I see.

"Well," he says, glancing at Mary and my mother, and then back at me. And I struggle to remain polite. "Mr. Little and I were standing at the sow's pen. Little's oldest girl was inside the cabin mending a mountain of trousers. His second girl and the two babies were out in the yard combing flax. We heard 'em coming through the woods. There was but a hair's breadth to act. Little ordered me and the girls to the house. He took off for his musket hanging in the barn. He thought he could make it. If he'd been younger, he just might have. But an older man like him, well," he says, shaking his head. "They sprung from the trees, painted and screechin' like a flock of wild turkeys. And it was done."

Done?

Mr. Little is dead?

"When they . . . got to him, those two small ones started screeching. I tell you, it was nothing like I ever heard before, those babies crying. I pulled 'em all inside and slammed the door. But I didn't know what to do next. I didn't have me a musket. It was Lizzy, the second of Little's girls, who had the idea for me to creep up the chimney. I didn't think I'd right fit, but I did. We all figured that there being no other men, they'd leave the girls in peace. Sarah, Little's oldest, stood guard in front of the hearth, holding onto those two babies whimpering into her skirts, when they burst through the door. There was many a man that came in, for I heard a load of shufflin'. And those poor little creatures started right back up with their shrieking." He wipes his mouth with his large-knuckled hand. "Strong girls, Little's two eldest, with sensible heads on their shoulders. I never heard them girls speak a word excepting to the crying babies. And I never heard no word spoken by the Indians or them Royalist rats. Then they left. Just like that. They gathered up the cows, the mule, and God knows what else, and left. I stayed all squeezed up there until the babies quieted. Creeping down was a mite harder than creeping up, I tell you." He smiles, wearily. And then turns to look out over the treetops. "He was a good man," he says, not taking his eyes from the tree line.

"He was a good man," my mother repeats softly. "And thanks be to God that the girls weren't left alone and had you there with them," she adds.

He turns back to us and pats my mother's arm. And then he tells us the part that I don't want to know.

"I had the girls stay in the cabin while I made pretense of checking for safety. Truly it was to drag their father's body into the barn. It would have been too much for the babies to see him that way. It was a bad sight . . . a bad sight . . . for

60

they scalped him, you know." He shakes as he remembers.

My mother wraps her arm under his. "And your wife?" she asks, changing the subject. "How does she fare?"

"She's been put through the mill, she has, but she fares well. She stayed behind with the girls while I came looking for you three. It's a terrible day, a terrible day for this valley." And he clings to my mother for support.

"It is, Mr. Van Etten," she soothes. "But let us start off for the girls and your wife. They'll be filled with worry until we arrive."

The four of us stagger south. The sun is beginning to set. The sky is an incredibly dark red. We walk in silence, each of us turning to his or her own thoughts. What will I say to her? Not one parent gone now, but two.

When we arrive, I'm not ready to see her, so I head for the barn. Although, this choice is not much better. I've never seen anyone scalped before. Putting it off, if only for another moment, I remove my frock and lay it neatly across the top of the leaching barrel outside the barn door. Taking one last long breath, I enter the barn to do what needs to be done.

I find him right where Mr. Van Etten said he placed him. I'm struck by how little blood there is. The scalp was taken so cleanly.

"Ah, Mr. Little, you look as though you've worked too hard today and have lain down in the hay for a rest," I tell him. If only this were true. Walking to the back of the old barn, I find one of the horse blankets folded neatly in an empty stall. After shaking it out, I lay it next to Eliza Little's father and roll him gently onto it, wrapping it tightly around him. I sit down heavily next to him in the hay and look up at the barn rafters. "I'm sorry that I didn't have time to know you better, sir," I tell him.

"It is a great loss," comes a whisper from behind me.

I jump up and turn, reaching for her without thinking, but I freeze solid when she stiffens. We stand like this, waiting for the arm's length that separates us to feel safe again.

"You can live with us," I say.

She lets out a little laugh. "You have no home, Noah Daniels. Your mother says that they have burned it down."

I grunt. She's right.

We're quiet again. I see her eyes find the rolled-up blanket at my feet.

"I'm going to plant wheat," I tell her. "Acres and acres of wheat. For the rest of my life."

What a beetle-headed thing to say.

Her eyes fill with tears and I watch as the shape of her familiar smile forms across her mouth.

"And maybe one field of corn," she says, as she reaches out across the space between us and catches the middle finger of my right hand in hers, squeezing it, releasing it, and turning to leave, all in one motion.

"Just one," I call after her, curling the chosen finger into my palm to feel its extra warmth. "And just to feed the pigs with," I add.

CHAPTER EIGHT

THE LONGEST NIGHT
THURSDAY, JULY 22, 1779

I prepare the wheat field in spring, turning the soil. The day I plant the seed is cool and wet. The sky and the river are the same shade of gray.

Scar gives a snort in his sleep and I start awake. Or at least I think I do—I must have been asleep if I can't remember my thoughts.

It's late. The sky is black, with no hint of dawn's glow. How can it still not be morning? This has got to be the longest night of my life.

I wiggle closer to Scar. Though my face and chest blaze hotter than the fire end of a flip-dog, I am frozen to the bone. And this dark, endless night makes me feel even colder. Thanks be to God that the burn in my belly has become more of a dull, faraway ache. Perhaps this means I'm beginning to mend. Or perhaps I'm just used to the pain.

I settle in and listen to the whistling of Scar's breathing. I wish I could hear his story. It's Scar's turn to bore me into release from this place.

I try to bring Eliza Little's face into my head, but I can't.

I toss things about in my memory, searching for her. I see the rock where we first sat together. I see the pines along the path where it curves down toward our farm. I even see her worn moccasins. But not her . . . I cannot see her.

CHAPTER NINE

I WILL GO

TUESDAY, JULY 20, 1779

I stand in the barn where she left me. I don't want to move
but I must. I need to get to Van Auken's Fort and check on
the rest of our settlement. I don't want to know any more
of the damage done today . . . any more of what might have
been prevented. But there is no avoiding it.

As I cross the dark yard, the Littles' cabin looks hot and
uninviting. When I open the door and step inside, I find the air
thick and stuffy, just as I suspected. Mrs. Van Etten is in the
middle of telling the story of her afternoon. I take a seat next
to Mary on a bench, knowing I will need to wait until she's
finished before I leave. Mary leans on me absentmindedly.
I let my eyes close as if I'm resting, but really it's to keep
from seeing Sarah and the little ones huddled together in a
ball of skirts and grief over on the bed. I try not to shift
uncomfortably as I listen to the old woman's voice.

"When I heard the hollering, I ran deeper into the woods.
I was so frightened being alone." Mrs. Van Etten breathes
heavily, as if just recalling her story is taxing her. "But I got
all turned around and I didn't know which direction to run,

so I just kneeled down and threw my apron over my head and closed my eyes tight. If I was to die today, I wasn't gonna watch it comin' at me. And so I sat there on my knees with my face buried in my apron and my eyes shut and I waited for death. Finally, I heard it coming for me, and I prayed to God Almighty for deliverance. But instead of that devil doing his deed, he knocked me to the ground, and I just laid there in the dirt shaking like I had me a fever, my head waiting for the blow of the tomahawk. But it never did come. What did come was a licking. Someone was licking my neck. When I finally found the courage to strip the apron from my face, I saw that it was Little Jo, the calf I'd been caring for. All along I thought I was being summoned to appear before God and it was that silly little cow that had gone and found me. Oh, Lord, I can't tell you how I praised God's name and hugged that calf." She wipes her eyes on her apron. "And Mr. Van Etten stuck in that old chimney . . ."

Mr. Van Etten hugs his wife gently. Poor Mrs. Van Etten. Attacked by a cow.

I give Mary's shoulder a little squeeze, and stand up. My mother sees that I need to speak to her and she makes her way over, joining Mary on the bench. "I'm leaving for the fort," I tell her. She nods. She will allow it. It's necessary that someone from our group report in at the fort, and if that choice is between Mr. Van Etten and me—the old man and the cripple—the cripple wins. "I'll be back by morning."

Mr. Van Etten meets me at the door. He shakes my hand. I can see Eliza Little out of the corner of my eye, sitting on a chair near her sisters, watching me. Her eyes shine brightly by the light of the fire, and the cabin is too tight and hot to bear a moment longer.

Outside, the night air cools my face and I breathe it in deep. I hated being in Mr. Little's cabin. It felt wrong—all of us sitting around without him. I remember that after he'd recovered from his illness and was able to attend church, he always chose the pew in front of me, Mary, and my mother. He liked to tell my mother each Sunday that as soon as they were completely settled, they would have us over for tea. I look around Mr. Little's farm and think back to the first time I walked Eliza Little home. It is an old place and needs work, but now I see he had cleared the paths, built strong fencing, split and stacked a good deal of wood, and had nearly all his wheat cut and bound. He worked hard, and for what? I turn and hurry west toward Van Auken's Fort, leaving this sad thought to wander alone like a ghost in Mr. Little's fields.

Not long after starting out, I pass the path leading home and can't stop myself from picturing the moon shining eerily on my burnt-out cabin. Then I see it in my mind's eye as it once was, its familiar shape against the night sky. The thought makes me unsteady, so I focus on the path in front of me and walk on, not raising my head until I smell the smoke from the Van Fleets'. It's not too far out of my way, just a short hike to the north, and I decide to turn toward it. I already know that it's been burned.

And it is.

To the ground.

Its blackened walls no longer resemble the house which stood on this spot my entire life.

I call out.

No one answers.

A chill settles on me and I quickly turn back for the fort. "Please, let the Van Fleets be well. Please, let no one else be hurt."

The last stretch of the hike feels like an eternity, which is not long enough. After what has happened to Mr. Little, my home, and the Van Fleets, I dread what I will find. So when I come upon the fort and see it's been untouched, I allow myself a few moments of relief before I walk on.

Van Auken's Fort is more like a strongly built house than a great fort like my father described Fort Stanwix to be. Despite its small size, Van Auken's Fort can fit a large portion of the inhabitants of our settlement. And tonight, as I walk inside, I'm sure it's where I'll find most of them.

Jon Haskell greets me at the door with a nod. It's quiet and cool inside. I hear soft crying and the shuffling of many bodies trying to get comfortable. One man's deep voice is speaking in a low tone to a group of men in the corner. I start toward them, but waver. The responsibility of reporting in at the fort had felt right on the walk here. Even my mother had allowed it. But now, as I'm about to approach the men, I think about my foot and imagine I don't belong.

I hang in the shadows and search the group of men for Mr. Decker, but I can see he's not there. Although I do spot

Martinus Jr., Mr. Decker's youngest boy, sitting close to the fire and playing with what looks like two coins. I watch him for a few moments. He's attempting to spin both coins at once. Martinus Jr. is only eight years old, but he has always seemed older. He's an outgoing and talkative boy, very much like his father.

I make my way over and sit. "How now, Martinus?"

"I am glad to see you, Noah," he says, acknowledging me but continuing to play at his coin-spinning.

"Where is your father?" I ask, bracing myself for the possibility that Mr. Decker is dead.

"Father's not here," he replies.

I bow my head in relief.

"He traveled south a few days ago. But mother said that Thomas Manning has gone to find him and bring him back." He stops spinning the coins and looks up at me. "Mr. Haskell sent John Carpenter out to look for you and Mary and Mr. and Mrs. Van Etten."

"He must have gone first to the Van Ettens'. I missed him. We've been at the Littles' this evening. Mr. Little is . . ." And I stop.

"Dead, Noah?" he says. "Mr. Vaneken is dead, too. They shot him on the schoolhouse steps. I ran when he told us to. He told all us boys to make for the woods. Unlike with our letters, he didn't have to tell us twice. I hadn't gotten but ten rods when I heard the musket. I knew it was Mr. Vaneken they kilt. My sister Emily said the girls rushed out to help him but it was too late. She said that one of the men stopped the others from hurting any of the girls on account of Brant's orders. Mr. Tyler says it was the Mohawk Joseph Brant they were talking about. I ran home, but they'd kindled it, so I ran here." His story finished, he looks down at the two coins sitting in the palm of his hand.

"I'm glad you're safe, Martinus." I pat his shoulder—but I think it's more for my own comfort than his. I stand to leave. I really should join the men now.

Martinus sits up and stares at me full in the face, and I'm overcome with the need to say something more. "It'll be all right," I tell him. But I don't know if it will be all right; in fact, it doesn't feel like it will be. And when the boy continues to talk, I know that it won't.

"They stole the Van Eck boys. Mr. Van Eck went after 'em and I heard them say he's dead. Mrs. Van Eck is quiet now, sleeping over by the Gilberts—," he motions off to a dark corner, "—but she screamed straight through dinner. I thought my hair would fall out of my head she screamed so loud. No one could stop her screaming. She sounded like a pig, half butchered . . ." His voice gets stuck.

"Be calm, Martinus," I say, sounding as if I'm looking to comfort him when I'm really attempting to stop him from saying anything more. It doesn't work.

"Mr. Packet is dead too. They shot him running to the fort. He almost made it. They scalped him just a few yards from the door. If you want to see him, Noah, he's lying covered up behind Mr. Cuddeback. I saw him. He looks the same except the top of his hair, skin and all, is cut off. I don't think it was much of a scalp because Mr. Packet was mostly bald, you know." And he shrugs. "Will you go see him?" he asks.

"No, Martinus." I back away. I need to join the men. It's time. But his small voice keeps on.

"They sent John Gilbert and Joseph Harper to Goshen for help. They're planning to chase down Joseph Brant. Will you go, too, Noah?"

The question throws me. I haven't thought about what happens next; my head is still stuck on today. I can't believe they took the Van Eck boys. Abram and Daniel are around the same age as Martinus Jr. And Mr. Van Eck, dead. Poor Mrs. Van Eck. She was already a sad and tired-looking woman. I think about Mr. Vaneken and Mr. Packet . . . and then me, buried under those branches.

"I must go, Martinus." And I know that I must.

"Yes, Noah," he says, lying back down on his stomach and returning to his coin-spinning.

I feel poorly leaving him, but I don't belong at the hearth with children playing games. I'm ready to join the men.

Mr. Tyler is speaking, but he nods in my direction when I step into the group. He's a rough man with eyes like two rocks. He doesn't live in our settlement. I'm not really sure where he lives. He seems to travel up and down the river on endless errands. He has a reputation for behaving rashly, but also for being outspoken for the cause. I've heard that before the war, he ran secret information between towns and settlements for the Committee of Safety, a respected group of men who worked for the new Continental Congress. Having anything to do with the Committee meant sure death if the British caught you.

". . . at least a few hours before daylight," Mr. Tyler says with authority. "Let's use it to collect any ammunition and muskets we can find. We should gather food and water for the trip as well. Hopefully, the militia will arrive sometime in the early morning and we'll start north."

"You can't be thinking of following him yourselves?" questions Mr. Jacobson, a young farmer with a large family who lives northeast of our settlement.

Mr. Tyler stands silent for a moment, as if not fully understanding what this farmer has just said. Once Mr. Jacobson's words register, Mr. Tyler's eyes glow with anger.

"Of course we are," he snarls. "They headed upriver and we'll head right after 'em, as soon as the militia shows up." He glares around at each of the other men, checking to be sure that this diseased thought of poor Mr. Jacobson's hasn't infected anyone else.

No one says a word.

"Me and Abraham will lead the way. We know that part of the country better than anyone and I'm in the mood to kill a few savages." Mr. Tyler almost dances as he speaks, unlike his friend, Abraham Cuddeback, who stands next to him barely blinking an eye.

The group is silent as we each consider what Mr. Tyler

has just said. Chasing after an experienced Mohawk warrior is not something any of us were thinking about when we rolled from our straw this morning.

Mr. Tyler keeps up his cold stare at the group, but his eyes seem to linger on me. I feel my face redden as I think back to the ditch. It's like he can see me lying there . . . hiding. And I wonder if, when these men hear of Mr. Little's death, they will realize that it could have been avoided if I'd run ahead to warn everyone. Perhaps even the Van Eck boys could have escaped being kidnapped. But then I wonder something worse . . . Maybe these men will take a long look at me and note sadly that I couldn't possibly have done anything to stop any of it.

In this moment, I gather the whole of the raid's horrors and throw it on my shoulders. And in a steady and strong and sure voice, relaying none of my actual feelings, I say it.

"I will follow you."

"The cripple's a fighter," Mr. Tyler booms. I bristle at his choice in words. They're the truth. But they still burn.

I hear the rustling of Mrs. Decker's buntlings before I see her. She hurries over to the group, elbowing her way in. She's a short, heavyset woman whose countenance is forever frozen in a scowl. My father used to say that Mr. Decker's farm yielded more beans than any other in the settlement because Mrs. Decker went out to the fields and, with a dark look, dared those pods not to produce. "Noah," she huffs, "you're staying right here."

It seems there's not a woman in this settlement who doesn't think she can order me about. "Ma'am," I say, too loudly, "I will follow Mr. Tyler and Mr. Cuddeback north."

Frowning, she turns to Mr. Tyler. "What have you to say to this, sir?" She crosses her arms and waits.

I reply before he can. "Mrs. Decker, my father believed strongly in this struggle for liberty. He fought for it on many occasions. Therefore, I know he would be proud to see me doing my part. I also know that he'd want me to help bring the Van Eck boys home."

"But, Noah . . ." she says, glancing pointedly down.

My earliest memories are of people's eyes finding my foot. I used to wonder what their thoughts were when they looked at it. Later I began to make up these thoughts for myself—none of them good. But right now, as Mrs. Decker's eyes find my foot, I don't do either of those things. Right now I just react. With anger. "I will refrain from battle if you think it best that someone with my . . ." I don't finish that sentence. "But Mrs. Decker," I say slowly, "make no mistake, I will be marching out with the militia."

Mr. Tyler chuckles. "He talks big, this one. Let the cripple come if he thinks he can keep up. It will do him good to see a little action, eh," and he punches me in my shoulder with his fist, almost knocking me over. "Maybe we'll let you scalp old Brant himself once we catch him."

Mrs. Decker isn't prepared for my heated speech or for Mr. Tyler overruling her, and before she can recover, Mr. Tyler is quick to forget about her. "Let's get moving on the ammunition, the food and water. Who's still missing? Anyone from your neck of the woods, boy?"

"The Van Ettens are at the Littles' with my mother and sister. Mr. Little was shot going for his gun. He's dead."

"That's too bad. He was a nice fellow," Tyler says. "Anyone else?" No one says anything. "Then we are down four good men today."

Quietly, in my head, I add the two boys.

The group breaks up. I make a wide circle around Mrs. Decker on my way out of the fort and start for the Littles'.

Once I'm alone again in the dark, I remember my mother. Getting past Mrs. Decker is one thing, but getting past my mother will be quite another. "Mr. Tyler said I could go" somehow sounds childish, and it won't stand up against my mother anyway. If she isn't behind the idea, and she won't be, then it doesn't matter if the Almighty Himself is behind the idea. I certainly can't use my father's zeal for the cause, because my mother doesn't share it, not then and not now. And if I bring up how proud Father would be, pretending to know his feelings on the matter, I would be sending any hope I had of my mother listening to me straight up the chimney.

My stride slows. It's as if my feet understand the danger in moving me closer to my mother while my head is still far from forming a convincing argument. Although as I listen to the steady rhythm of my footsteps, the inevitable confrontation with my mother fades and is replaced by a vivid daydream of fighting the British.

I have loads of these stories of glory stored in my head, thanks to my father—different ways where my quick thinking or sharp shooting turns the tide in a decisive battle. I choose one of my favorites to replay in my mind. And in what feels like no time at all, I'm back at the Littles' farm.

The edges of the world are beginning to lighten. Morning is on its way. I haven't slept all night but I feel more awake than I ever have in my whole life.

And I know exactly what I must do.

CHAPTER TEN

OH, YES, FREEDOM

THURSDAY, JULY 22, 1779

Scar breathes noisily, asleep beside me. I stare straight into the darkness of my eyelids, concentrating hard. At home, this sometimes works and I drop off to sleep. It isn't working now, even though I'm so unbelievably tired. Probably because Scar is sleeping so . . . loudly. My father was also a loud sleeper. He would snore and toss and turn all night. I think we sleep like we live, and my father lived and slept noisily.

Reaching out, I pick up the sleeve of his hunting frock. I bring it to my nose and breathe my father in deep, shivering as I release my breath. My body is on fire, yet I feel colder than the water in a washbasin on a February morning. Why am I here? Why did I want to join this fight?

I remember the walk to the Littles' on my way back from the fort the day of the raid. A tight bitterness pulls at my chest and I toss the sleeve to the ground. "This is not like your stories, Father," I spit.

He answers me in the universal response of the dead—silence—and the rage at the sound of it nearly splits me in two.

I jerk my head from these thoughts and turn toward the

Indian snoring next to me. Knotted scalp lock . . . dark lashes resting on sunken cheeks . . . lips turned down in a loose frown . . . Not a single line crosses his brow. He would be dying here alone in the woods had I not come.

The anger runs out of me like dry soil through my fingers. It's no use now anyway, and I don't have the strength for it.

Scar shuffles his legs, stirring up the leaves underneath. His eyes flutter and his eyelids open just a tiny crack. "Noah?" he whispers.

"I'm here," I tell him. "Go back to sleep."

His eyes close.

"Wait!" I call. All of a sudden I need to know. "Your name. What's your name?"

I see his mouth turn up in a small smile. "Scar," he mouths. Then the smile fades and he's again lost in sleep.

I laugh, quietly. So like Eliza . . . he mocks me. And now the ball, the heat, the cold, the scratchy dead leaves, I feel none of them.

He's snoring again, this time a little louder than before.

I listen to him sleep . . . and begin to drift off. I remember that he was my enemy once. Scar. A healed wound. His new wound is not going to heal. Do the wounds of war ever heal, leaving only a scar where we once all bled? My head feels thick and heavy, as though stuffed full of deer hair like my moccasins in winter. His real name. I need to know it. To remember. And feeling unhappy and confused, I pass from wakefulness to sleep.

I watch the plants produce new stalks, or "tillers." The young wheat is strong and green. The moist days of late spring make the plants happy. A good crop can grow two heads taller than a man, and this one is on its way. It tickles my chin as I walk through the rows.

CHAPTER ELEVEN

MEN OF FLINT OR EATERS OF MEN

WEDNESDAY, JULY 21, 1779

I head straight for the barn to hunt for Mr. Little's musket. I've determined to follow the militia without warning my mother, and I'd like to do so with a musket in my hands. I'm positive the raiders have taken it, but I look anyway. It doesn't feel right marching out of the settlement without one. Not that I know what marching out feels like, with or without a firelock.

I've never been out of the settlement. That is, if you don't count the few miles around our cabin to check traps. I try to imagine the march north—which leads me to imagine those we'll be marching toward. They're up there . . . somewhere. I picture the Mohawk warrior who is probably right now pestering my pigs to pick up their pace, and I'm reminded of something my father told me long ago: that the word *Mohawk* is the Algonquin name given to these people and it means "man-eater." Their real name, the name they call themselves, is *Kanien´kehaka*, which means "flint people." I wonder who we will be chasing, the men of flint or the eaters of men? And to which group does Joseph Brant belong?

Brant is definitely a man to be feared. He's a veteran warrior, and his cruelty in battle is well known. But there are other stories, too, those that tell of his great intelligence and of the risks he takes to save settlers from being scalped or burned. He seems more legend than real.

But then I remember Mr. Little lying dead not ten feet from me. Brant is real.

I find a small lantern and light it, but I'm so unfamiliar with this barn that I don't know where to start looking for a musket, balls, or powder. I'm just roaming around aimlessly, putting off the decision I've already made: returning to the fort without speaking to my mother. But then I see it, sitting on the leaching barrel outside the open barn door where I'd forgotten it yesterday evening. My father's frock.

My father would have marched out with the militia. He never backed down when it came to serving in this war. He loved calling us Americans, instead of Colonists. "His Majesty's subject?" he would spit. "I am no man's subject."

But then my mother's face fills my head. That hard look in her eyes. It shouts the reason why I shouldn't go—I am lame, maimed, a cripple. Although my mother has never once allowed this fact to keep me from tilling fields, splitting wood, stacking wheat, mending fences, rebuilding outbuildings, topping corn for the livestock, weeding and weeding and weeding, and all the other endless work that keeps me busy from morning to night, every day of every week. These tasks I can do. But enter the war? My mother's logic is off and she knows it just as well as I do. What holds me back is not my mother, and it is not my foot . . . What holds me back is me.

I will go. I will keep my word to Mrs. Decker and stay out of the fighting so my being lame hurts no man, but I will go. "Don't let others shoulder a responsibility that is yours," my mother has told me many times. Well, this is my responsibility. Brant attacked us. He attacked me. He burned my home. He killed Mr. Little. It is my responsibility.

Blowing out the lantern, I hang it on the nearest peg and head over to the frock and put it on. The smoke from the Littles' cabin catches my eye. I watch it curl from the chimney.

"I'll be back in less than a day. Two days at the most," I whisper.

CHAPTER TWELVE

TIRED

THURSDAY, JULY 22, 1779

In midsummer, flowering begins. The kernels are soft but dry. The dark green plants begin to fade. Soon they will explode into a golden amber. The time for harvest is near.

An elbow jabs my arm.

Where am I?

Ah, yes. Here. With Scar. He's sleeping . . . fitfully.

I close my eyes and listen to the whip-poor-wills calling to each other overhead. Or are those mockingbirds just pretending to be whip-poor-wills? Mockingbirds love mimicking other birds. I whistle the three notes of a chickadee, "Dee, dee, dee," and wait. The mockingbirds whistle back, "Dee, dee, dee," making me smile. I will rise soon. I will rise and pick up my grass sickle and finish edging this cornfield.

Scar mumbles.

But first I will help Scar.

I'm lifting his head to give him a drink from the canteen when I jerk awake. I'm not in my cornfield and I'm not helping Scar. I'm dreaming. And thirsty. And soaked through with sweat. I open and close my eyes several times, trying to unglue myself from this strange world between dream and reality. But when I try to move, fever rushes to my head and I give up, dropping back onto the soft earth with a sigh. I'm tired. Too tired.

"Scar." It hurts my head to speak.

"Noah." He answers from far away, though his body is lying next to mine.

Moving to comfort him, I catch hold of a piece of his shredded shirt, and then I slip back into sleep and away from him . . . or he from me.

CHAPTER THIRTEEN

IT'S A DANGEROUS THING THAT WE PROPOSE TO DO

WEDNESDAY, JULY 21, 1779

The sun rises over Van Auken's Fort as I approach it for the second time. Between yesterday's stay in a ditch, losing Mr. Little, and the hike back and forth to the fort, all I want is to relieve my neck from the weight of my head.

I enter the dark fort. All is quiet. A thin ray of sunlight sneaks through the chinking. I lie down in it on the hard, cool floor, close my eyes, and sleep . . . but not for long.

Martinus Jr. discharges his imaginary musket way too close to my tired head. "You're awful quick to reload, Martinus," I yawn. "I would think it would take longer. It takes me longer."

As if to impress me, he lays the invisible musket on his lap, opens the cartridge box, bites off the end to expose the powder, dumps it into the pan of the lock, slams shut the pan, drops the cartridge into the barrel, rams the rammer, cocks the lock, and presents his musket to the enemy, discharging the imaginary ball with such a roar that—even knowing it was coming—I jump.

"Good shot, Martinus, I think you got him."

"I did," he announces without emotion, because there

had never been a question in his mind that he would. "Mr. Tyler asked for you, Noah," he says, reloading.

The militia is here. I'm awake and on my feet faster than a flash of summer lightning. As I pass Martinus, he catches the hem of my frock.

"What's wrong, Martinus?"

"Don't go, Noah."

He won't look at me or release the frock.

"Martinus," I say, bending down on one knee. I try to get his eyes to meet mine, but they won't. "I'll be back in a couple of days. I'm going to bring Abram and Daniel home."

There is the sound of many hooves meeting hard dirt.

I disengage his grip.

"Martinus," I call to him as I walk backward toward the door of the fort. "I'll be home soon." But he still refuses to look up. I turn to leave, telling myself that as soon as this is over I'll spend some time with him. My mother's voice repeating one of her favorite sayings invades my head: "Do it now, later never comes." But at that moment the hum of a hundred voices drowns her out, and I hurry to see the sight.

And oh, what a sight it is! There are horses and men everywhere; it's as though General Hand and Count Pulaski are back. Only these men are not in uniform. General Washington has no money to outfit the militia. My father liked to say, "A man can fight just as long and just as hard wearing his undergarments, if he has a mind to." The memory of his loud laugh echoes through me and I smile. "I would be sweating far less right now, Father, if I were in my undergarments," I whisper. And sweating I am, though the sun has barely had a chance to creep past the horizon.

My eyes search for Mr. Tyler and I find him across the road talking with a small, thin man who wears leather boots and a waistcoat. I can tell from the look on Mr. Tyler's face as he listens to the man that he respects this small fellow. For one, Mr. Tyler is usually the person doing all the talking, but now he stands motionless, letting the man speak. I'm curious, and start off toward them, but I'm distracted by the crowd . . . the glorious, beautiful crowd. Men I don't know, horses everywhere, voices ringing out all around me, and Joshua. Joshua? What is he doing here?

"Josh!" I call. But he can't hear me over the mass of people and animals. Forgetting about Mr. Tyler, I head for Josh.

Joshua is a hat maker from New Jersey who is not much older than me. We met a few years ago when he stopped in our settlement for the night on his way north to visit relatives. My father struck up a conversation with him out in front of Patterson's Sawmill, and invited him home for dinner. Josh was a Patriot down to his stockings, and he and my father were friends almost immediately. He had a great sense of humor, and like my father, he knew how to tell a story. He never failed to make us laugh.

The story I remember most was about a man who had come in for a hat and asked Josh for his very best. I try to remember the man's name. It was a funny-sounding name—Meeker, that was it, Mr. Meeker. When Josh showed

Mr. Meeker a hat, it seemed to please Mr. Meeker in fit and style but surprised the gentleman by its low price of five pounds. Josh immediately understood that the man believed the hat inferior due to its low price, and took the five-pound hat back into his workshop, brushed it thoroughly, and then presented it to Mr. Meeker as a ten-pound hat. The gentleman quickly purchased it. What a great laugh we had at this poor man's expense.

After this, Josh regularly stopped at our house on his travels north. But it had been a long while since I'd seen him. He'd been busy, off fighting in the war.

"Josh," I call again. Before I can reach him, he sees me and bounds up the road. Grabbing ahold of me, he lifts me off the ground in a hug, shouting into my face, "How fares my old friend, Noah?" Laughing, he drops me, holding onto my shoulders to keep me steady. "How does your father? Is he here?" He spins around in his moccasins with a big grin on his face.

What wouldn't I give to turn and see my father walk out of the press of people around us. My heart, so light a moment ago, feels as heavy as a hogshead full of ale. "Josh . . . ," I say, searching for the best way to tell him—but there is only one way. "Josh, my father has passed on."

His smile vanishes. We say nothing to each other for a few moments, and then Josh claps me hard on my back. "We'll get those Tory scum, Noah," he growls.

"It wasn't them, Josh. He died of illness over a year ago. I should have written. I'm sorry," I tell him.

"No problem, old friend," he says, steering me by the shoulders to a shady spot alongside the road. We sit on the grass. He opens up his jacket to pull out a handkerchief and slowly wipes his face. He is taking in my awful news as he looks off into the crowd. I follow his gaze.

"Who is the man in the boots talking with the rough-looking fellow?" I ask, attempting to direct our thoughts away from my father.

"You mean Dr. Tusten? He's from Goshen, New York, about twenty miles southeast of here. He's in charge of this underdressed army today."

I look around at us all milling about in the hot sun. Every one of us looks like he's just gotten in from plowing.

"They say that he's a magician when it comes to healing people," Josh says. "I met a boy who told me that Dr. Tusten stuck him with a needle full of pox to keep him from dying of the sickness. Doesn't make sense to me, but I'm just a hat maker." He looks over at me. "I'm real sorry about your father, Noah."

I can't return his gaze. "Thank you."

Josh and my father were a lot alike. They shared that lightness of spirit I wish I had. They both moved through life with ease. Life doesn't allow me to pass so easily. Most days, it seems, I have to fight my way through it.

We're quiet. Josh's eyes stay on me. I keep mine pinned on the dusty road before us. Men are exchanging information about the raid or discussing what will come next. A few women stand near, not speaking, babies on their hips and worried looks on their faces. Children dart about between them, not realizing the seriousness of the situation. There is one particular fellow sitting atop a fine-looking horse and causing a small commotion as he tries to dismount in the center of a group of men. He has the largest nostrils I've ever seen, larger than the nostrils of the horse he rides.

"Who is that?" I ask.

"That's Major Meeker from Sussex County in New Jersey," Josh says. "He is commander of the Sussex troops that came in a few moments ago." Josh rolls back onto the grass, closing his eyes. He places his arms behind his head.

"Meeker? The buyer of the hat, Meeker?" I ask.

Josh laughs out loud, keeping his eyes closed. "What a memory you have, Noah," he says. "Yes, Meeker of the hat." He fishes out his handkerchief again and wipes his face. The heat is already oppressive.

"Tell me about yesterday, Noah."

I sigh and stretch out next to him. "They came in around dinner time. My mother, Mary, and I ran to the ditch I dug after the raid on Peenpack." My face colors with shame as I repeat my sin of hiding in the ditch, and I'm glad for Josh's closed eyes. "They came from the north—at least, I think they did. I couldn't tell how many there were, or how many Indians and how many Tories, since they were all dressed as Indians with their faces covered in war paint. They burned down our house and barn, and then took off south. From what I can tell so far, they burned about four or five houses and about the same number of barns, and I heard the church is gone, as well as two of our forts and the sawmill up the road. They wounded one man—shot him right off his horse—killed four others, and kidnapped two young boys. Mr. Tyler says they headed north, directly up the Delaware River. And with all the animals and supplies they stole from us, he thinks they can't be moving too fast. He plans on catching them by marching us up the Cushetunk path, which also leads north, but inland from the river."

"Us?" questions Josh, opening his eyes halfway and looking at me without turning his head. "I didn't think your mum would allow that."

Before Josh can see the pain he causes me with those words, Mr. Tyler appears above us. "Boy, I need you to come with me."

"I'll be right back," I say, without looking over at Josh. I'm happy to leave him in this manner.

Mr. Tyler leads me toward the doctor. As we approach, he looks up, and I hide my limp while at the same time hating myself for doing it. Never once do the doctor's eyes look down.

He reaches out and shakes my hand. "I'm right heartily glad to meet you, son. My name is Dr. Benjamin Tusten." His hand is strong but soft; he doesn't pull a living from the soil.

"How do you do, sir?" I say. "I am Noah Daniels." And I look to Mr. Tyler, wondering why he asked me to come meet this doctor.

"Boy," Mr. Tyler begins, and I can see he's in his usual serious mood, his eyes jumping from me, to the doctor, to the crowd in the road, and then back to me again. "You're to stay with this man for the duration of the campaign. He's a Lieutenant Colonel and the commanding officer. And since you aren't part of the formal militia and you aren't a guide, where he goes, you go. That is, if you're still coming with us." And with that said, he walks away.

"Yes," I call after him, trying not to shout, "I'm still coming."

Dr. Tusten stands quietly. The men, the horses, and the dust seem not to touch him. Calmly, he watches me. If I'm supposed to say something, I don't know what it is.

"I hope that your family and home are well after yesterday's attack," he says.

"My home was burned, but my family is well," I answer.

He nods slowly, still watching me. He is taking me in; he is taking in my foot. I can feel it. I want to tell him that I'm able. That I can join this fight. And that I'll fight for the same reason as any other man here: freedom from England.

"Noah, it's a dangerous thing that we propose to do," he says, reading my thoughts. "This man, Joseph Brant, is not to be taken lightly. He's a serious opponent. I will stand before these other men in a few moments and tell them the same thing I'm telling you. General Washington should have the chance to hear about the raid, and we should wait for reinforcements before we go running up the river." He gestures to the scene before us, at the dust-choked road and the farming men hanging about it. "There aren't many of us, son, and there are even fewer of us with experience to match Mr. Brant's. You could stay behind. You're . . . young," he finishes.

I wince at his last word, understanding its true meaning.

In an instant, I see this great mass of men moving upriver without me. And I see myself, trudging back to the Littles' farm and proceeding with the cutting of hay and the chasing of loose cows.

"Dr. Tusten," I say, trying to find the steady voice that Eliza Little told me I possessed. "If I were to ask these men sweating in the hot sun right now, each of them would own a good reason to stay behind, just as you believe I do." I wave over at Mr. Jacobson. "That man has six children to feed. And the Reverend has a portion of his flock to put to rest after yesterday. And Jon Haskell's wife is sick with fever." There is no shortage of pain and suffering in the lives of poor farmers, and I could have gone on, but instead, I turn back to him. "And you, sir, you're standing here before me, even though I'm sure that you must have a wife and children to think about. I will follow this militia, Dr. Tusten, whether you agree with my decision or not, sir."

And though I desperately want to turn my head away from him and calm myself, I stand as still as I can, trying to wear that look of determination my mother has worn on her face all my life.

The doctor doesn't speak right away. "Let's gather the men and talk," he says, finally. "We need to discuss our next move. You know what I think. Let's see what these good men here have to say." He turns and walks off toward the front of the fort. And I follow.

Within a few moments we're all assembled around the palisade. Josh joins me, and there is no more talk between us about what my mother will or will not allow me to do.

Dr. Tusten raises his hand for silence and begins to speak.

"We have a decision to make," he says with force, but not loudly. The men quiet. The women move off to the side of the crowd, huddling in their own little groups, and the children, sensing the change in the hush of the crowd, take their games up the road toward the blacksmith's. What is truly unbelievable is that at this very same time yesterday morning, I was busy worrying about how I would cut, gather, and dry two crops of hay this summer instead of our usual one, due to all the rain in June. And here I am today standing in the middle of a road I've walked down all my life, surrounded by a group of mostly strangers, listening to a man I just met discussing whether or not we will run upriver after the infamous Joseph Brant. It all seems unreal. Except for the sweat rolling down my back—that is real enough.

I squint through the sun at the doctor. "As you all must know," he says, "Joseph Brant came through this settlement yesterday. We believe he is proceeding north along the Delaware River. Do we follow Brant directly, or do we wait for others to join us? I say wait."

The groans are loud. The crowd that had been respectfully subdued is now alive. The men turn to each other in anger and disbelief. This is not the speech they had assembled to hear—not the fiery beginning of revenge on Brant they had all ridden into the settlement expecting. The grumbling grows and I immediately feel a need to protect this doctor, to defend him. But he stands in place, allowing the men to continue their outburst, without even so much as a shift of his weight from foot to foot.

Eventually, he puts up his hand to quiet us. "Hear me out, and then I shall hear you out."

We settle down, but there are a few angry voices scattered here and there among us that take their time, and the doctor waits patiently for them to stop. "None of us possess much in the way of supplies or ammunition. Look around at one another, and think of what you yourself carry."

Not a single head in the crowd moves, but all of our eyes check out our nearest neighbors.

"Second, we know that our enemy is Joseph Brant, a formidable foe against any number of men, and we have reason to believe he is in command of a large number. We are not more than one hundred, my fellows. So I put it before you: Do we follow at this time, or do we wait for reinforcements?" He folds his hands in front of him as if he's just finished telling us something pleasant. And like that moment between hot wax striking your skin and the pain flaring, we stand without reaction.

But not Mr. Meeker—Major Meeker. He is up on his horse. "We came to fight, not to wait about for those who may or may not arrive." His nostrils flare, and spit or sweat—

I cannot tell which—flies in all directions. "This settlement has been ravaged, burned, beaten, and robbed. Be it Joseph Brant or the Devil himself, let us go after him," he shouts, as his angry eyes search the crowd for others who would kill the Devil. And those others exist, because they begin to howl and pound their firelocks at the blue summer sky.

Again, the doctor raises his hand and calls gently for silence. "Think, my friends. Waiting for ammunition, supplies, more help—it might not take as long as you believe, and it could mean a world of difference if we do engage the enemy."

But the crowd is done listening to this small man standing on a patch of dried grass in front of a stake wall. He cannot compete with the wild-looking Meeker yelling from atop an excited horse.

"*If* we engage the enemy?" cries Major Meeker. "We *shall* engage him, my good doctor, and we shall *run him down*. He will not need to wait for our revenge; we will bring it straightaway," he vows, shaking his fist toward the north. "Let the brave men follow me. The cowards may stay behind."

And with those words, the roar of the men assaults my ears. This is what they have been waiting for. This was the spark needed to light the vast kindling assembled in their collective hearts. But why is it that when our hearts fill with emotion, our heads empty of good thought? I watch Dr. Tusten through the sweaty and excited crowd. He doesn't move. He seems not even to blink. But I see thoughts cross in front of his eyes, and I feel apprehension rise in my throat.

What does this modest doctor know that I don't? But maybe I know it, too.

I take a long look around at us all. Our numbers are few. And most carry a single sack that must include all the food, water, and ammunition in our possession. We wear coarsely made waistcoats over grass-stained shirts, with worn-out moccasins on our feet . . . or none at all. We resemble a gathering of farmers, not military men, which is exactly what we are. And more than a few of us are way beyond the appropriate age for a soldier.

I try to think back to the voices of the men I heard burning down my home. How many were there? And what kind of men follow a man like Joseph Brant?

CHAPTER FOURTEEN

DON'T LET GO
THURSDAY, JULY 22, 1779

My fingers ache from clutching the rough fabric of Scar's shirt, but I don't let go.

The beautiful shhhhh *of the wind blows through the wheat.*

No. There is no wind.

Everything is still. Scar is still. Too still.

Shhhhh. Yes. Be still.

I can't clear my senses. But I don't want to. I close my eyes and slide back into a dream. There is the rocky path. The dark hemlocks. The marching men. And Josh. Not the cold, crumpled Josh I tripped over in the smoky heat of battle—but the chatting, laughing Josh who walked upriver alongside me yesterday.

Was it just yesterday?

CHAPTER FIFTEEN

THE MARCH NORTH
WEDNESDAY, JULY 21, 1779

The militia moves north.

After Mr. Meeker's triumphant speech in front of the fort, no one had ears for anything else Dr. Tusten had to say. I might have been the only one who heard his last supplication to the crowd—"I shall go as far as you will, but I shall not compel one of our men to go." And now I feel as though I'm carrying those words on my back along with two of his knapsacks. He attempted to hand me his lightest. I chose his heaviest.

We march past Martinus Decker's burned-out fort, and turn toward the Cushetunk path. Our neighbors line the road. They watch us pass with long, tight faces. No one waves, steps from the crowd, or calls out a name. I look for Mrs. Decker, and am glad when I don't see her.

Once we are clear of the settlement, a few farms dot the landscape, but the cabins are far off and there is no sign of the inhabitants. The doctor's warnings seem to echo in the stillness . . . small numbers, low supplies. But then we enter the shade of the woods. The air cools, the men begin to chat, and my head clears of worry.

We don't achieve a great distance before Colonel Hathorn of Warwick, New York, joins us from the southeast with about thirty more men. He takes command over the doctor.

The cheerful colonel improves my mood even further. He is easy with the men. And as we push our bodies through the steamy summer day, he keeps up a long stream of amiable talk. I labor to continue in his company so that I may listen.

There are about a hundred and twenty of us—militia men from Sussex, New Jersey, to the south of our settlement, and Goshen and Warwick, New York, to the east. Together we march north under the dark branches of the pine and hemlock. The Cushetunk path leaves the Delaware a mile or so out of the settlement and winds itself uphill into the forest, after which it turns and heads north again, parallel to the river. The plan is to stay on this path until we are aligned with Brant, and then march on a bit farther, where we will loop around toward the river and come down on our enemy from the north, a direction he won't be prepared for.

It's a rocky climb, treacherous for the horses, who need to be walked, but also for us, as we must pay close attention so as not to turn our ankles on the loose stone. The air is still and wet with heat, and our frocks and shirts are dark with sweat. The path itself is shaded, and without the thick, green branches to protect our heads from the sun, I don't believe any of us could keep on like this. I see how much my daily walks have conditioned me as I watch the other men struggle. We march on and on without rest, but I'm determined that nothing will bring my spirits down: not the heat, not the pace, and most especially, not my foot.

Our guides, Mr. Tyler and Mr. Cuddeback, lead our troop. Dr. Tusten follows next. He doesn't speak to anyone and no one seeks his company, except for Colonel Hathorn now and then. Following the doctor is the colonel. After listening to the colonel tell tales of his life for many miles, I fall back to find Josh walking toward the middle of our line.

Josh is where the fun is. A man named Solomon is telling stories of his enlistments. It seems he has traveled everywhere, though he can't be much older than Josh. He's lived in the city of New York, repairing gun batteries, and in New Jersey, mining iron for making steel. I envy him his many journeys. They might not seem far to some, but for me, who has never even ventured down this path leading away from home, visiting the city of New York might as well be a trip across the sea to meet King George himself. One moment, Solomon has us laughing at a poor drunk soldier who can't find his tent on a dark night, and the next, he has us wondering if anyone will survive when a fire breaks out in a gun foundry. But then the conversation turns to women.

The path gives me an education, although not one my mother would approve of. A tall, heavyset man named Daniel Myers leads this line of talk, yet many heartily join in. I can feel Josh's eyes on me. He's wondering whether he should move me along. But you're either in or you're out—and Josh lets me stay in. The farther up the path we march, the more fantastic the stories become. But this doesn't matter. It's all in fun, and the laughter is real. And the arm that Josh throws around my shoulder is very real.

More men join as the discussion rolls on into the afternoon. They have much to add that makes my face burn hotter than the midday sun. I soon leave, and head to the front of the line, chewing on a piece of ashcake with a goal to make it last.

When I catch up to Dr. Tusten, his smile is so friendly that it feels natural to walk beside him. We huff along next to each other for a while, listening to the other breathe. I can feel him wanting to ask how I'm doing. The truth is, the day's march is adding up. With every step, the question weighs heavier on my mind: *How much farther will I be able to go?*

It's like the doctor hears it, and in response he begins to talk. "I'm a farmer's son, just as you are, Noah," he says. "Raised only thirty miles from here."

I glance over at him—taking in his pleated coat, his leather boots, his neck stock—and although I mean no disrespect, he quickly understands that I don't believe him, and laughs.

"It's true, son. I grew up on a farm along the banks of the Otter Kill." He takes in a long, slow breath through his nose. "And I can still smell the mud of the swamps in August and taste the roasted corn . . . the boiled corn . . . the corn pudding . . . the corn porridge . . . the corn and beans."

Now we both laugh. He *is* a farmer's son.

He describes his family's farm outside of Goshen, bordered by the shady Otter Kill, with its rolling hills and mossy banks. "But my body was small and I was often sick as a child, so my father had me concentrate on my studies. And when I was twelve, he sent me away to apprentice a doctor."

I'm too tired to hold back my bold question. "Are you unhappy with your father's choice?"

He's quiet for a moment, and I begin to stammer an apology, but he interrupts.

"No," he says, slowly. "I'm not unhappy with it, Noah, and I'm sure that I do more good this way. But," he sighs, "there are times when I wish I could belong in both worlds, farming and medicine."

His honesty brings out my own. "Farming is all I know," I tell him. "But for longer than I could handle a plow I've wanted to belong here . . . in this war."

I quickly find out that the doctor enjoys speaking about the war much more than he does about corn pudding or doctoring. We hike past a forest of pines while he explains the failed British strategy to divide the middle colonies away from New England—it seems the British believed those of us in the middle colonies would be easy to defeat, since we're swarming with Tories—and then, with us out of the way, they'd be able to conquer our Patriot brothers in New England and the war would be over. But we were stronger than they thought, which the doctor's long tale of the battle of Saratoga proves. Most of his story I'd heard before, but today, marching alongside these men, panting alongside them, every word sounds new. The doctor may have been apprehensive about chasing after Joseph Brant, but he is certain in his patriotism.

"The British fight with their pride, Noah," the doctor says. "We fight with our hearts. And pride tires much faster than the heart. The heart is a miraculous muscle. It receives its power from an unknown source, and the more action you send its way, the stronger and harder it beats. King George will have to send over more than his pride to stamp out the heart of this war."

Dr. Tusten glows with sweat from his passionate speech and our endless marching. I give him a moment to catch his breath and then ask, "So what happens next?"

He shocks me with a loud burst of laughter. "You are what happens next, Noah," he laughs.

I grin. I'm happy to be walking with him . . . happy to listen to his talk . . . happy to be marching and fighting. I can almost hear my father joking with the men behind me. I fight the urge to turn . . . to look for his face. Because I know he isn't there.

Dr. Tusten grows quiet with his own thoughts, perhaps about his family or maybe about what is to come ahead on the path. I want him to keep talking but I can see he's done for now, so I leave him there to be alone, dropping back by easy measures to join Josh.

My head feels like I've drunk too much mulled cider and I can barely feel my legs. I let the other men overtake me by twos and threes. Someone I don't know claps me on the back as he passes. Another man, in the middle of a sentence, turns to nod at me as he moves by. I catch tiny pieces of conversations . . . fall planting . . . musket care. The long snake of men keeps me moving forward as it winds its way past me. The darkness is deepening, yet I feel light and awake. I'm fighting for what my father wanted. I'm fighting for what I believe in. I'm fighting with my heart.

But our enemy crawls into my head and I can't get him out. What is Joseph Brant fighting with? Maybe he fights because he's bound by the Covenant Chain, the treaty between the six nations of the Iroquois and English that unites them like brothers. Maybe he fights because he considers himself English. I've heard he's actually sailed to England and met the king and queen.

I stumble along behind a man whose form I can barely make out in the dusk and think about Joseph Brant . . . about all the Indians. They once populated this land we're marching through, but not anymore. It has become my father's land. And Mr. Little's, who traveled all the way from Connecticut to claim it. Even mine, with my dreams of what I will do with my own farm one day. Maybe the king promised Brant that he'll stop the Colonists from snatching up the land . . . that if England wins the war, he'll fence us into New Jersey, Massachusetts, or Connecticut. I wonder if Joseph Brant believed him.

I slide in next to Josh. We walk, silent, except for the slapping of mosquitos from our necks. I force myself to match his stride while I push thoughts of Joseph Brant and Indians and land and everything else out of my head, and fix my attention on the sound of feet crunching forest floor. It seems we've been marching since God created Adam.

I hear Major Meeker behind us. He's lingered near the back of the group all day. His loud wheezing seems to fall into rhythm with our footsteps. He's a big man and the heat and rapid pace must surely have affected him greatly. He urges the men: "Come on boys, we'll catch 'em yet, put yer heart in it."

I smile. I like the pompous major with his gigantic nostrils and his expensive hat.

"Yes, boys, put your heart in it," I say quietly as we march on into the night.

CHAPTER SIXTEEN

NOTHING

FRIDAY, JULY 23, 1779

I hear something. A rustling? A movement? I cough . . . causing white spots of pain to light up behind my closed eyes. My temples throb as my ears suck in every sound around me. But all I hear is my own raspy breath.

"It's only a dream," I mumble, licking at my dry lips. Where is the water?

But wait . . . I hear it again . . .

The last leaf hangs low on the stalk. Is it ready?

"Father?"

I open my eyes.

"Scar?"

He doesn't answer.

I turn my head toward him and end up with a bunch of his thick, black hair in my mouth.

Again I hear it. A whisper.

I breathe in . . . and out . . . in . . . and out . . . trying to quiet the thudding of my heart.

The sky is brightening. I can no longer see the stars.

It's nothing. I close my eyes.

But then my eyes fly open. I have not heard a sound, but deep inside, I feel it.

He's coming.

CHAPTER SEVENTEEN

A SHOT CRACKS THE SILENCE

THURSDAY, JULY 22, 1779

We marched all day and long into the night, camping finally after the moon had a good view of us. The miles added up to more than twenty, and my good mood disappeared into the sticky July night. My body is a tangle of aches this morning as I hobble into a clearing.

More pine, more rocks, more laurel . . . from the view around me, I could easily be within shouting distance of home. But the white faces of the tired men who file into the clearing after me transform it into an alien place. They sag against trees, collapse in patches of ferns, and drain their canteens, but no one makes a sound.

The day has dawned bright, not a cloud in the sky. But the heat hammers away at us, morning or night; there is no relief from it. My clothes itch and I would do just about anything to dive into the cool river right now. I wipe the sweat from my face with my sleeve. We're getting closer. There is no more laughter, no more claps on the back. Joseph Brant. His men. They're not far from where we're standing. Abram and Daniel, the two stolen boys, come into my mind. I attempt to imagine their feelings this morning but then stop. There is no sense to thoughts like this.

Out of the corner of my eye, I see the doctor and the colonel gather with Major Meeker and a Mr. Wisner, who is a Lieutenant Colonel. I make my way over to the doctor's side, as I was given an order to stay close to him. The four men speak in low voices.

"Do we continue?" Dr. Tusten asks. He doesn't look at Colonel Hathorn, but squints out into the hemlock. It's as though he's trying to hide his thoughts so they don't interfere with the colonel's decision.

"Of course we do," spits Major Meeker. The major has no trouble letting his wishes be known, and he elbows poor Lieutenant Colonel Wisner in the ribs to bring the fellow round. The lieutenant colonel rubs his ribs and agrees with the major.

Colonel Hathorn studies the ground at his feet.

Major Meeker begins to speak again, but the doctor puts a hand on his arm to stop him. "Let him think," Dr. Tusten says.

I can see the major struggle to keep silent. Still, Colonel Hathorn does not look up or respond.

Maybe we won't catch up to Brant. Maybe it will all end in this clearing. How would I feel if this were true, and if our little army were to turn for home right now? I look behind me at the way we came, through the trees, south, toward my mother and Mary . . . toward Eliza Little.

Colonel Hathorn interrupts my thoughts.

"We have come for a fight and we shall show Joseph Brant and these Tories a fight," he says quietly, still not meeting the company's eyes.

Major Meeker beams.

"Let us stick to our original plan," continues the colonel. He turns to Dr. Tusten. "Benjamin, you will attack from our right flank, Lieutenant Colonel Wisner will charge the left flank, and I shall strike from the middle. But first we shall proceed up the path, looping back to surprise them from the direction they least expect, the north."

If Dr. Tusten disagrees, I see nothing in him that says as much. He promptly hands me the rest of his extra medical sacks and begins to head north on our path. I gladly follow him.

The doctor and I lead the line, behind Tyler and Cuddeback, who have gone ahead to scout out Brant's exact position. I keep my eyes locked on the doctor's back.

We are moving fast. I follow too closely. When I fall, I don't feel the pain of my knee against the rock, just the warm blood seeping through my trousers. When I stand, I step on one of the knapsacks and trip again, winding up back in the dirt. The doctor gives me his hand, but I refuse it, and I stumble up and after him.

I see nothing but the fabric of the doctor's jacket. My own breath fills my ears. The medical bags crowd around me. It's just as yesterday, I tell myself, we are only marching . . .

marching . . . marching. After a few paces I begin to relax.

A shot cracks the silence.

We freeze—as if that single musket ball has stopped every one of us dead in our tracks. The shot is followed by a volley of three or four more. These bring us instantly back to life and we scurry about like ants that have lost their trail.

This is not in the plan.

Dr. Tusten shouts to those of us assigned to him and then motions us downhill toward the river. Again, I follow him, forcing myself to keep back so as not to knock him down from behind. He turns to find me and I run into him, losing my balance. His hands grip my shoulders and he yanks me back to my feet.

"Noah." He shakes me, not hard, but so that he has my attention.

I nod. I'm with him.

He releases me and heads west again, but slower, his gaze scouring the trees. We're no longer a large group, but more like thirty or forty. Josh and I acknowledge each other with a look.

Silence.

Slinking.

Every step forward. Unbearable.

Ahead . . . movement.

Men.

The enemy.

I do as the others do, and drop to my belly behind a rock.

The explosion of musket fire fills the forest.

I pull my legs in under me and crouch behind the rock with my eyes pressed shut and my forehead against the cool stone. My nose fills with musket smoke. I open my eyes. The smoke burns and I can't see a thing. A body bangs into mine, knocking me into the pine needles. A musket is thrust into my chest by a man I recognize, but don't know by name.

"Load it," he growls.

I do as I'm told. He snatches the musket from me and shoves a second one at me. I reload it and hand it back to him, retrieving the first musket to load again. Sweat and smoke squeeze in around us and all I see is the man, the rock, and the musket I load.

Fill the lock, drop in the cartridge . . . ramming, cocking, until my whole body knows the routine and performs it in swift, fluid motions. I crouch behind the rock and reload over and over and over.

I start to feel almost comfortable. There's nothing like having a task. It's my mother coming out in me. I even let myself look around a little. Dr. Tusten is not far off through the smoke, firing and reloading, firing and reloading. I can see other men now, crouched like my partner and me behind their own rocks or trees, firing and reloading as we are. I stretch just a little to look around the rock and I swear I can feel a musket ball pass through my hair. I will not do that again.

I return to reloading.

I don't know how long we've been behind this rock—long enough for me to memorize this spot on earth for life. A rough piece of the rock juts out a little and catches my elbow as I reload, sending sparks of pain through my arm. I will die here, and the last thing I'll see is this small piece of forest. I forget to hand over the musket and my partner yanks it from my hands, catching my finger . . . more pain.

I pick up the musket he dropped and reload. I certainly don't need two good feet for this.

I'm so thirsty that my tongue feels like it doesn't belong to me. And the smoke is roasting my eyes from my head. How is my partner standing this?

He peers over the rock, stiff, aiming. I watch him wait patiently for a target. He's a calculating shot. Thanks be to God for this, as it gives me more time to reload. I can't tell if he's hitting anything or not. Of course, I'm hoping he is.

He's a tall man, but thin. Although he must have a solid constitution, for he hasn't taken a moment's rest since the firing started, and not once has he investigated his whereabouts. He must have been here before, in battle, crouching and endlessly firing into a black cloud of smoke. I itch inside my father's frock. I would be far less sweaty if I removed it, but I know that I won't.

Reload, reload, reload. The sun has passed overhead, and if our shadows were visible through the smoke, they'd be growing in length.

I dream of water—the way the river looks frozen over

in winter with large chunks of ice bobbing in the center, the day it poured rain with the sun still shining when I was out plowing, every wasteful splash I ever let slide over the side of my water bucket.

Reload, reload . . . smoke and this rock. "Please, God, let this stop," I pray.

But then my prayer is answered, and I immediately wish to reload a hundred more muskets against this rock than be forced to leave it.

Someone howls down the line to my right. I can't see who it is, but his howls sound like an animal caught in one of my traps. My partner fires his musket and throws it my way, taking off like a rabbit in the direction of the injured man. Dr. Tusten jumps in behind me on my left and shoves me hard into my partner's position behind the rock.

"We're down men, Noah. You'll have to start shooting," he shouts directly into my ear, his breath hotter than the muggy air, and then he crawls off after my partner and the injured man.

I clutch the loaded musket. And then I turn, point, and pull the trigger. There is no thought about a target. I just have to fire off the first shot. The crouching and reloading are over, replaced by the new series of crouching, reloading, and firing.

A cheer rises up from the enemy. It's so loud. It's so close. How many of them are out there? Have they received reinforcements? Following the cheer—there comes the most grotesque sound I've ever heard coming from fellow human beings. It is some sort of guttural song or chant, which ends with more terrifying shouts of joy. I sit, fixed behind my rock, clinging to my musket.

"Shoot, Noah," I tell myself, but I can't move. The terrible whooping fills my ears. I cannot move.

Dr. Tusten scrambles back behind my rock, shouting at me to carry the packs and muskets he drops at my knees. I don't want to give up my rock. There is some kind of safety here, some kind of loyalty I feel toward this spot. But before I can protest, Dr. Tusten disappears into the smoke, only to return a moment later dragging someone I assume is the wounded man I heard howling. He isn't howling anymore; in fact, he looks dead.

"Follow me, Noah," Dr. Tusten yells, commanding me with his dark eyes. So I pick up the muskets and packs and trip after him as he stumbles backward through the woods, hauling the wounded man over leaves and rocks and branches. I stay hunched over, but each time a musket fires, I crouch down even closer to the earth until I feel like a snake slithering along behind the doctor. If only I could move like this, sliding on my belly, I'd do it. The packs and muskets are weighing me down and I half drag, half crawl right over top of them.

We aren't the only ones on the move. Many of our men are retreating with us. This doesn't seem like a good sign to me. Distracted by this bad thought, I trip over a soft obstacle, falling on top of it. It's Josh.

"Josh! Josh!" I scream into his face, violently shaking his shoulders. He doesn't respond.

I stick my head into the air . . . creating a perfect target for the enemy. "I need help! I need help!" I scream, again and again. To anyone. "Help! Help!" To no one. "I need . . . help."

But it's no use.

No one can help.

He is dead.

"Dr. Tusten," I whisper, defeated.

The doctor is struggling with the weight of the wounded man up ahead of me. He looks back and motions hard with his chin for me to keep up.

But I can't leave Josh. I won't leave Josh. I throw his musket over my shoulder with the others, grab his knapsack along with the doctor's, and try dragging him from under his armpits the way I see the doctor moving the wounded man. Josh isn't large and my arms are strong, but the sacks and muskets are falling all over the place and slowing me down, and with each loud crack of a musket, I drop to my knees. The hollering. The whooping. It weakens me. This is useless. I know it. But I keep dragging him because I don't know what else to do. The doctor runs back and grabs me, pulling me and my sacks and muskets away from Josh. I don't fight him.

Hot sweat burns my eyes and the taste of salt wets my tongue.

Dr. Tusten throws me behind a new rock and begins to tend the wounded man. I can't move. I lie with my face in the dirt. It smells sweet. I see my mother bending over a row of corn seedlings, weeding. But then she kicks me. No, it's the doctor. He's binding up some poor fellow's shattered leg and glaring at me. "Get up, Noah, and help me," he orders. "Now! See how I place the wad of dressing over the bleeding? This will put pressure on the wound and stop the blood flow. Noah . . . watch. See how I wind the bandage around to apply the pressure on the wound and keep it clean?"

"Is he dead?" I ask.

"If he were, Noah, I wouldn't be dressing his wounds. He has just lost consciousness. Listen, I'm off to search for others, stay here and load the muskets." And he's gone.

I do as I'm told, and load. My arms are so sore from this task that they feel clumsy and odd. Before I have the second musket loaded, Dr. Tusten returns with another screaming man.

Blood, sweat, screaming, death . . . "Put your hand over here, Noah, and push down," more screaming, and grunting, and moaning. The moaning is worse than the screaming. The moaning is so much worse.

More of our men gather around us. I can see them behind trees and rocks, loading . . . firing. Through the smoke comes the shrieking. It seems to reach out and grab me by the throat and squeeze, slowly. It sounds closer now.

"Noah, here, roll this around the splint, like this . . ."

I roll the bandage around the bloody arm of some poor fellow.

"Now, tie it here, off the site of the wound." Dr. Tusten

comforts the injured man with one breath and instructs me with the next. It is better to move in this way, to follow him, than to think about what is happening around me.

I'm in the middle of wrapping what is left of Jon Haskell's knee when I catch sight of Colonel Hathorn coming in on our left. He looks like a different man from the man he was this morning; his bright eyes are cloudy and his clothes are wet and crusted with dirt and leaves. He meets the doctor's eye and then drops behind a rock and begins to load. He comes up from the rock and aims south, not west, which is the direction we've been shooting in all day. Has the enemy moved?

But that thought is quickly put to rest. I hear the cries of our enemy coming from the south now as well as the west. And a few moments later, I hear their howling coming from the east. We are hemmed in.

I can see our men scattered throughout the forest. But we don't number that many. I count us up . . . and have to stop at around thirty, including the wounded lying at my feet. Where is everyone? They cannot be dead. That would be over a hundred dead. They cannot be dead. I grab at Dr. Tusten's elbow. "Doctor, where is everyone? Why are we so few?"

The doctor continues his work for a moment, and then stops and says low into my ear, "I don't know, Noah, we've either lost heavily or some of the men have been cut off from us. Keep tending the wounded and stick close to me.

They need us, and it's all we can do right now."

I return to my cleaning and wrapping and calming. But I'm not calm. The sky feels as if it's pushing down on me, and I'm holding it up with my shoulders. As I work, more men drag themselves near the doctor and me, and we're running out of cover. The musket balls bounce off nearby rocks and trees, spraying us with pine needles and dirt. The doctor sees this, nods at me to keep working, and takes off.

I feel frantic without him. I can't remember how to do anything. The man in front of me is bleeding from a small musket hole in his shoulder near his neck, and compared to some of the grisly wounds I've encountered today, his seems small and unworthy of my time. I move onto the next man, but the man with the hole in his shoulder catches my wrist. I look down at him. "Yes, yes, I'll be right there," I tell him. But when I turn back, he's dead. Where is the doctor?

Dr. Tusten dives back behind our rock and begins to gather up our supplies. "We're moving. There's a rock ledge behind us where we can tend the men better. It's good cover and lots of it." He tells the men who can still walk to follow us, and the rest, that we'll return for them one at a time. We don't need to explain why.

Again I follow the doctor, banging my knees on rocks, the sacks snagging every fallen tree branch I crawl past. He disappears over a small ledge and I slide down after him.

"Stay with these men while I return for the others," he shouts as he climbs back up and over the ledge. It's the farthest I've been from musket fire all day, but I don't relax, not with the wounded surrounding me. I begin to clean, wrap, and calm them. I know all of their faces, and a few of their names. One of the men stops me and tries to hand me something. He struggles to speak, and his voice comes out almost too thin to hear.

"Give this—to my wife—please—and—tell her—I loved her—to the end," he says in short gasps. I run my eyes along the top of the ledge, searching for the doctor. He's nowhere in sight. I can't do this without him. The man coughs, long and wet.

"No, sir," I say, as I gently squeeze his arm, refusing to take whatever trinket he's trying to give me, "you will have to love her longer, I'm afraid." He laughs silently at the joke that I hadn't meant to make and it relieves us both.

The doctor calls from above, "Noah, grab him," and he slides a large man down the pebbly edge of our ledge. The man is mostly unconscious and doesn't take notice of his precarious position. I catch him under his arms but can't hold him, and he hits the earth hard, crying out, "My leg, my God, my leg!" I open up his stocking and find such a mess that I stare at it, wondering what to do. The doctor interrupts my attempts to stop the leg from bleeding with another wounded man to catch off the ledge . . . and after that, another.

"Dr. Tusten," I call, but he's gone again.

I'm beginning to wonder who's left fighting up there.

I rush back and forth between the men, feeling lost. The doctor finally slides down the ledge, and in one breath's time, has cared for most of the small wounds, and a few of the large ones. I thank the Lord. I could not have lasted one more moment without him. I duck back to work, wishing I had ten more hands to lend this doctor and these poor, hurt fellows.

Then I hear something, or rather . . . I don't hear something. I stop, trying to figure out what has changed, and in an instant, it hits me. The musket fire has slackened. I hear one pop. Two pops. But then nothing. Is it over? I turn to find the doctor. "Dr. Tusten!"

He's right behind me, his back to mine. "Keep working, Noah, I hear it," he whispers.

"What does it mean?"

My answer drops down our ledge. It's Colonel Hathorn, white-faced and out of breath. He picks his way through the wounded, and I can see that he's trying not to look at them. Some of the men recognize him. One calls out his name, and another reaches for him, but he skirts around the man's hand in his hurry to get to the doctor.

"Benjamin, it's over, they've broken through up at the northeastern end of our line. We couldn't hold them." His voice is low so as not to alarm our injured. "I don't know what happened to Lieutenant Colonel Wisner and his men. I haven't seen any of them since the first musket shot. We number only what you see here before you, and about twenty more men up atop the ledge." He fixes his gaze on the doctor and leans in closer to him. "I have released the men."

We've lost? I can't believe it. But I find that I don't care. No. I don't care. It's over. Oh, thanks be to God, it's over. We are released.

But the colonel's hard stare remains steady.

We can't be in danger any longer if we've lost? Surely they won't hurt the wounded? And then I realize that they can and they will. "But the Van Eck boys," I mumble. No. This is not how it was supposed to be.

"Benjamin," Colonial Hathorn whispers.

"Go," says the doctor. "And take him with you." He nods at me.

"I won't leave you." I don't even look at Colonel Hathorn. "I won't."

"Noah," Dr. Tusten begins, but he's cut off by the colonel.

"Follow me if you want to live, Noah," he says. Then he grabs the doctor's hand, shaking it . . . not letting it go. Perhaps he's never seen a hero before. I know what the doctor is doing right now is surely heroic. I only stay because I fear losing him. I've lost my father, and Josh. I can't lose him.

I feel the colonel look my way. I don't move. He turns to leave. The wounded men call out to him. It's a hideous sound . . . their begging. I weave in and out of them trying to give them words of comfort. But they will not be comforted any longer. They hear the howling of the enemy just as I do.

I watch Colonel Hathorn's back fade into the trees. But I know I can't follow him. And they're coming.

I don't look at Dr. Tusten, but keep moving from man to man, pretending to check dressings. But I see nothing. My ears hear only the shrieking and my sight has shut down. The doctor yells at me but his words have no meaning. He yells again and I look at him as if through a fog. "Noah, climb that ledge and find my other knapsack. I need more dressings RIGHT NOW!" he roars.

I scramble up the slippery ledge after the sack.

Once up on top, I search the forest floor but don't see it. The pines block out the sunlight so well that there's not much small growth on the forest floor, and I should easily have found the sack if it were nearby. But my eyes are useless, and my head swivels round and round on my shoulders, making me dizzy. I wander farther from the ledge. The sun is setting and I blink again and again, staring out into the darkening woods.

Then I see it! Ten paces ahead. I stumble forward, and as I bend to pick it up, I'm knocked over by something catching me in the side, throwing me to the ground. I lie facedown in the dirt, stunned, not understanding what just happened— until I feel the burning.

The shouts of the wounded compel me to leave the ground and head back to the ledge. I have the sack. I must return to the doctor. My side burns, and I have trouble standing straight . . . I half crawl toward the ledge.

Just as I near the spot where I climbed up, I see them come out from the trees in the opposite direction. I can't see my men below, but I can hear them shouting for mercy. Their cries fill me with courage and I leap up, ignoring the pain of the musket ball.

But Dr. Tusten is waiting. He's standing with his back to the Indians coming for him. He's scanning the top of the ledge. He's watching for me. His eyes find mine and before the first Indian can get to him, he gives me one last order: "Run!"

I watch him go down. They scalp him alive, although I hear no sound come from him. And then I follow his order and run like hell.

CHAPTER EIGHTEEN

KEEP YOUR PROMISE
FRIDAY, JULY 23, 1779

The sky is getting light. It's morning . . . finally. I try to lift my arms and shake him, but I only manage to push on his side. "Scar," I whisper. He doesn't answer. He's hard to the touch. "Scar."

I stare past the trees into the quiet morning light. He's left me. As my father did, and Josh, and the doctor. They are all gone. I am alone.

But not for long.

They arrive in silence, filling our small clearing. Staring, they surround us. I see them struggle to understand the scene before them, the two of us, side by side on our backs, bleeding into the hemlock needles. I see them recognize Scar . . .

"His name." The words sting my dry throat.

One of them steps toward us. He has wide eyes and a large forehead. His scalp lock is long, hanging well past his shoulders. He moves closer. Just like me, he is shiny with sweat and covered in musket powder. I know he's not coming to kill me—his face doesn't have that look on it, that horrible look I remember on the faces of Brant's men as they approached the wounded under the ledge. What then? Scar . . . he's coming for Scar.

"HIS NAME?" I shout, the strength of my own voice surprising me. And then I grab Scar, burying my face in the worn frock—and I wait for the Indian to rip him from me.

"Ronhnhí:io," a soft voice says. It is not a question or a command.

I look up. A tall Indian in deerskin leggings and a green military tunic emerges from the trees. A silver-mounted cutlass hangs at his side. It is him. Joseph Brant.

"His name. It is Ronhnhí:io." I watch him look down at Scar. "It means, 'he who has a good spirit.'"

The sweaty Indian retreats and I loosen my painful hold. He who has a good spirit. Yes. That is it. My head sinks back to the earth, and for the first time, I notice the cool morning air on my cheeks.

I want them to leave us now. I want them all to go. But they don't. They hang back. A few sit. One bows his head in prayer. I can hear his voice but can't make out what he's saying. It's like they've forgotten about us. Why do they stay? What are they waiting for?

An emptiness spreads through me . . . I realize what they're waiting for. I know. I'm not going home.

I look around at the men, searching for a way to be wrong. But I can't make out any of their faces, except one. Joseph Brant. When I catch Brant's eye, he's not uncomfortable with it and keeps my gaze. He moves closer, kneeling at my side.

His moccasins, those white beads, the red tassels . . . the same ones I saw from under the laurel branches three days ago.

My eyes are too heavy and I let them close.

. . . Water. I need to get to the river. He's standing in the middle of the wheat field.

"Scar!" I shout. "Are you thirsty?" He doesn't answer. Instead he waves to me, just as the bearded heads of grain wave to the clouds gliding across the high summer sky. "Wait!" But he's already turning—already racing away through the straw-colored wheat.

I jerk awake. And I know that I'm alone under the frock before I even open my eyes. My friend is gone.

Brant makes me drink. I want to refuse, but I'm too thirsty. He places my head back onto the ground and waits. Scar died with me by his side and now I will die with this man by mine. But the thought doesn't comfort me, and with him sitting so close, so quiet, I lose my courage to die silently, as I know I should. "I lost . . . we lost." I'm embarrassed at my stammering, but the expression on the Mohawk leader's face doesn't change.

He looks up, as if through a hole in the cloudy morning sky. He's silent, staring through that hole. And then he looks back down at me and smiles a weary smile, drained of happiness. "Boy, I fight a battle every day of my life that I know I will lose."

"Is it worth this?"

At first his face slackens. But then a hardness takes over

his features. "It's not that the fight is worth your life, it's that your life is worthless if you do not fight."

I see in an instant the fight Brant speaks of, and its hopelessness. Not the war between the British and the Colonies, but the fight for his own freedom and the freedom of those who have followed him into the clearing this morning to find Scar and take him home.

Freedom.

Wasn't that the same thing I was fighting for?

My mother's face and Mary's tinkling laughter float over me, and then Dr. Tusten's kind voice: "You are what happens next, Noah" . . . so tired . . . and then her . . . shaking my hand, telling me that two days make her wiser.

Eliza.

The thought of never seeing her again shreds my heart like a battlefield of musket balls. The sadness is suffocating, and I'm afraid . . . so afraid.

"Wheat," I tell him, but I can't make out his face anymore. "I promised."

He bends close to my ear. I feel his warm, comforting breath on my forehead—or is it my father's breath? "Go keep your promise, boy."

And I slip away under my father's old blue hunting frock.

Epilogue

On a sunny Tuesday afternoon in July, Joseph Brant, under British orders, descended on the settlement of Minisink (the present-day city of Port Jervis and the town of Deerpark, New York) with twenty-seven Tories and sixty Iroquois, where they plundered, burned, and killed.

Loaded down with stolen supplies and livestock, Brant took off north as fast as possible, taking the path along the Delaware River.

Word of the destruction spread and the militia responded. By noon the following day, Lieutenant Colonel Benjamin Tusten and Colonel John Hathorn, with 120 men gathered from New York and New Jersey, marched upriver in pursuit of the Mohawk leader.

Early the next morning, under the charge of Colonel Hathorn, the militia prepared to attack. But before the men were in place, a musket shot rang out. Captain Tyler had gone ahead to scout the exact whereabouts of Brant and his troops. Some say, upon discovering them, he accidentally discharged his musket. Others say he unwisely shot at one of

Brant's men crossing the river. Tyler was killed on the spot, his reason for the shot forever buried in history.

With the element of surprise lost, the battle began . . .

The militia quickly divided into three divisions: Tusten on the right, Hathorn in the center, and Lieutenant Colonel Wisner on the left. Joseph Brant was a quarter-mile downriver when Tyler's musket fired. He immediately gathered half his men and started up the hill from the river. This maneuver brought Brant around behind both Hathorn and Tusten, completely splitting off Wisner's division. Wisner's men, accounting for at least a third of the militia, ran off, never to be heard from again, thus leaving Tusten and Hathorn behind to face Brant's experienced war party with only eighty men.

When Brant's party began firing on the rear of the militia, with the division he left at the river firing on its front, another large group of the militia broke and fled. Hathorn and Tusten were now left with approximately forty men hard pressed on three sides.

The battle wore on for hours, but the militiamen were eventually overpowered. Although casualty reports are not clear, it is thought that forty-seven militiamen and eight of Brant's men were lost that day. Brant carried away his fallen from the field, as was the Mohawk custom. No one was left alive to bury the bodies of the militiamen.

The dead would have to be patient. It would be over forty long years before anyone would come for them. The dangers of the war and the wild place in which they died kept their whereabouts hidden. It was not until 1822 that a scouting party finally found the scene of the battle. The bones of the men were collected and encased in two walnut coffins. And on July 22, forty-three years to the day they fought and died, all were buried in a mass grave in Goshen, New York.

All but one.

There is a legend that, near the battleground, entirely covered up with loose slate, was found the skeleton of a young colonial soldier. According to one nineteenth-century historian, "This was probably the work of the Indians, who for some reason gave this man a sepulcher."

The monument to the men who fought in the Battle of Minisink sits on this very spot today.

About the Characters

Dr. Benjamin Tusten—Born on December 11, 1743, in Southold, Long Island, to a family of farmers. When Tusten was still a young child, his family moved to Goshen, New York. Because he was a sickly child and unable to farm, his family sent him back to Long Island to go to school. He began his studies in medicine in Newark, New Jersey, and New York City. Dr. Tusten was one of the pioneers in the inoculation against smallpox in America, inoculating over 800 individuals. He joined the militia as a Lieutenant Colonel of the Third Regiment of Orange County, commissioned on February 26, 1778. He died at the Battle of Minisink on July 22, 1779. The town established on the land where he died is now named in his honor, the town of Tusten, New York.

John Hathorn—Born in Wilmington, Delaware, on January 9, 1749, he was a surveyor and a schoolteacher by profession. He moved to Philadelphia to further his education, and then from Philadelphia to Warwick, New York, to work as a surveyor. He became captain of the Colonial Militia and colonel of the Fourth Orange County (NY) Regiment in February 1776, and served throughout the Revolutionary War. Later he became the brigadier general of the Orange County Militia and major general of the State Militia. Hathorn was a member of the State Assembly, where he served eight terms and served as speaker in 1783 and 1784. He served in the State Senate from 1786 to 1790 and 1799 to 1803, and was elected to the Continental Congress in December 1788, and the First Congress in 1789. He was elected as a Republican to the Fourth Congress in 1795. On July 22, 1822, Hathorn, now seventy-three years old and a general, was present for the laying of the cornerstone of the monument to those who fell in the Battle of Minisink. John Hathorn died in Warwick, Orange County, NY, on February 19, 1825.

Joseph Brant/Thayentané:ken (his Mohawk name)—Born on the banks of the Cuyahoga River in 1743, Brant was selected by Sir William Johnson, British Superintendent of Indian Affairs for the northern colonies, to attend Eleazar Wheelock's Moor's Charity School for Indians in Lebanon, Connecticut—which, along with Wheelock's Latin School, later became Dartmouth College. Here he learned English and studied Western history and literature. Brant left school to serve under Sir William from 1755 to 1759 during the French and Indian War (1754–1763), and later became an interpreter in the British Indian Department. In 1775,

Brant made his first trip to England. When he returned to the colonies, he was a principal player in recruiting many Six Nations men for the British side of the Revolutionary War. After their defeat, the British awarded him land on the Grand River in Ontario, to which he led Mohawk and other Indian Loyalists (those Native Americans who had supported the British in the Revolutionary War) in 1784 and established the Grand River Reserve for the Mohawk. Brant again went to England in 1785, where he was able to obtain compensation for Mohawk losses in the Revolutionary War. Following this, he devoted the remainder of his life to the interests of his nation. Brant died on November 24, 1807, at his estate on Burlington Bay, at the head of Lake Ontario.

Bezaleel Tyler—Born on February 26, 1745, in Sharon, Connecticut. During the early years of the Revolutionary War, Tyler was living near Cushetunk, about thirty miles north of the settlement of Minisink. The area of Cushetunk was known to be loyal to England, and possibly this is the reason that Tyler was down near the settlement of Minisink at the time of the raid. He died at the Battle of Minisink on July 22, 1779. Many of his descendants still live in the area, where the town of Tylerville, Pennsylvania, is named for his family.

Abraham Cuddeback—Born in the Minisink settlement area known as Cuddebackville, which still exists today and is named for his family. Cuddeback's birth date is unknown. He was a farmer, mechanic, shoemaker, weaver, and tailor. He was known for his large size and great marksmanship. Cuddeback was very active in the Revolutionary War. He survived the Battle of Minisink, dying on August 25, 1817.

Samuel Meeker—Very little is known about Meeker. Neither his birth date or date of death has been recorded. He was said to be a farmer and a zealous Patriot, selling all he had to fight England. At the time of the Battle of Minisink, Meeker was part of the Second Regiment of the Sussex County Militia. He survived the Battle of Minisink and served until honorably discharged at the close of the Revolutionary War.

ACKNOWLEDGMENTS

Many thanks . . .

to Peter Osborne. You and "The Battle" are synonymous. You have been so very, very good to me.

to Mark Hendrickson, who leads a secret life that helped me write a book.

to Jon Inners, you rock (he is a geologist . . . just so we're all in on the joke).

to Frank Salvati. There is no other person on earth who I would rather listen to for hours on the telephone.

to Kaweienón:ni Cook, for your beautiful choice in names.

to Nancy Conod and Susan Breyer . . . the hardboiled egg is missing from this book just for you two.

to Konwanonhsiyohstha Hill, for not only being the fastest reader I know, but the most enthusiastic and thoughtful.

to Leslie Caulfield, Shari Becker, Sarah Cassell, Christine Carron, Heather Demetrios, and David Fulk. I'd join a pirate crew for you guys! And you know how I feel about sharks, large bodies of water, and the sacking of ships.

to Kevin Mann, Maria Hykin, and Jennifer Salvato Doktorski—my grandmother used to say that if you want to know who you are, check out the people you hang with . . . I am obviously amazing.

to Lisa Rosinsky, whose thoughtful comment saved my story. And to Carolyn Yoder, for there once was an editor (you) who saw more in me than I saw in myself . . . and then, like all great editors, she coaxed that story out.

BIBLIOGRAPHY

"A Look at Our Heritage: Tusten Bicentennial 1776."
Tusten Bicentennial Commission. 1976.

Angell, Pauline. *Fifty Years on the Frontier with the Dutch
Congregation at Maghaghkamik.* Port Jervis, NY:
Port Law Press, 1937.

Berland, Dennis, Patricia Valence, and Russell Woodling.
*The Minisink: A Chronicle of One of America's First
and Last Frontiers.* Four County Task Force on the
Tocks Island Dam Project, 1975.

Chalmers, Harvey. *Joseph Brant: Mohawk.* East Lansing,
MI: Michigan State University Press, 1955.

Clark, Donald F. "Joseph Brant and the Battle of Minisink."
Orange County Historical Society [Goshen]. 22 July
1972: 1.

Curtis, Mary. "1779: Hannah Thomas' Story." *The
Observer* [Port Jervis]. 30 Sept. 2002: 1.

Dutch Church Records of the Machakemeck & Mennisenk Churches. Port Jervis, NY: Deerpark Reformed Church, 1899.

Egger-Bovet, Howard, and Marlene Smith-Baranzini. *USKids History: Book of American Revolution.* New York: Little, Brown and Company, 1994.

Farlekas, Chris. "Brant's Raid Retraced: July 20, 1779." *The Times Herald Record* [Middletown]. 26 June 1979: 1.

George-Kanentiio, Doug (Kanentiio), *Iroquois Culture & Commentary.* Santa Fe: Clear Light Publishers, 2000.

Graymont, Barbara. *The Iroquois in the American Revolution.* Syracuse, NY: Syracuse University Press, 1972.

Gumaer, Peter. *A History of Deerpark in Orange County.* Port Jervis, NY: Minisink Valley Historical Society, 1994.

Hendrickson, Mark, Jon D. Inners, and Peter Osborne. *So Many Brave Men: A History of the Battle at Minisink Ford.* Easton, PA: Pienpack Publishing, 2010.

Inners, Jon D., and Peter Osborne. *Blood and Mayhem on the Delaware: The Historical Geography of Brant's Raid and the Battle of Minisink.* Port Jervis, NY: Minisink Valley Historical Society, 2001.

Kelsay, Isabel Thompson. *Joseph Brant, 1743–1807, Man of Two Worlds*. Syracuse, NY: Syracuse University Press, 1984.

Leslie, Vernon. *The Battle of Minisink: A Revolutionary War Engagement in the Upper Delaware Valley*. Middletown, NY: T.E. Henderson, 1975.

Letters to Sarah: A Year in the Life of a Settler's Family. Monticello, NY: Sullivan County Department of Public Works, 1989.

Meyers, Arthur N. "Colonel Tusten, Patriot and Doctor." *Delaware Valley News Times* [Tusten]. 26 Feb. 1970: 1.

Meyers, Arthur N. "Joseph Brant, Delaware Valley Visitor." *Delaware Valley News Times* [Tusten]. 21 Mar. 1968: 1.

Meyers, Arthur N. "Tragedy and Humor in Minisink Days." *Delaware Valley News Times* [Tusten]. 10 Sept. 1970: 1.

Osborne, Peter. *The Historic Markers of the City of Port Jervis and the Town of Deerpark*. Port Jervis, NY: Port Jervis City Historian and Port Jervis Area Heritage Commission, 1989. Updated through 2009.

Osborne, Peter. *The New York–New Jersey Boundary Line: While New Jersey Dozed, New York Was Wide Awake*. Port Jervis, NY: Minisink Valley Historical Society, 1997.

Osborne, Peter. "Remembering Lt. Martinus Decker: Perseverance & Vigilance During the War for Independence." *The Observer* [Port Jervis]. 31 Oct. 2002: 1.

Porter, Tom (Sakokweniónkwas), Lesley Forrester, and Ka-Hon-Hes. *And Grandma Said . . . Iroquois Teachings: As passed down through the oral tradition.* Philadelphia: Xlibris, 2008.

Quinlan, James Eldridge, and Thomas Antisell. *History of Sullivan County: Embracing an Account of Its Geology, Climate, Aborigines, Early Settlement, Organization; the Formation of Its Towns with Biographical Sketches of Prominent Residents.* Liberty, NY: G.M. Beebe & W.T. Morgans, 1873.

Richards, Mark V. *The Sesquicentennial of the Battle of Minisink: A Story of the Commemoration Held on the Battlefield at Minisink Ford, Sullivan County, N.Y., July 22, 1929.* Monticello, NY: Republican Watchman, 1929.

Seward, Dr. Frederick T. "Legends of Minisink Battle: 195 Anniversary of the Battle of Minisink." Goshen, NY: Goshen's Library and Historical Society, 1979.

Smith, Philip H. *Legends of the Shawangunk (Shon-Gum) and Its Environs, Including Historical Sketches, Biographical Notices, and Thrilling Border Incidents and Adventures Relating to Those Portions of the Counties Orange, Ulster and Sullivan Lying in the Shawangunk Region.* Syracuse, NY: Syracuse University Press, 1965 (reprint from 1887).

Stickney, Charles. *History of the Minisink Region.* Port Jervis, NY: Minisink Valley Historical Society, 1867.

Twichell, Horace. *History of the Minisink Country.* New York: Schilling Press, 1912.

Tyson, John R. *Charles Wesley: A Reader.* Oxford, UK: Oxford University Press, 2000.

Van Etten, Delbert. "The Battle of Minisink: 202 Years Ago Wednesday." *Sullivan County Democrat* [Callicoon]. 21 July 1981: 1.